SOUND FROM A STAR

NOVELS BY FRED YAGER

Cybersona
Rex

NOVELS BY FRED YAGER AND JAN YAGER

Untimely Death
Just Your Everyday People

Sound FROM A Star

Fred Yager

A NOVEL

HANNACROIX CREEK BOOKS, INC.
Stamford, Connecticut

2011 Hannacroix Creek Books Paperback Edition

Published by:

Hannacroix Creek Books, Inc.
1127 High Ridge Road, PMB 110
Stamford, CT 06905-1203

e-mail: Hannacroix@aol.com
www.hannacroixcreekbooks.com

Cover design by Susan St. Laurent

Interior Layout & Design by Scribe Freelance
www.scribefreelance.com

ISBN: 978-1-889262-99-4

LIBRARY OF CONGRESS CATALOGING-IN-PUBLICATION DATA

Yager, Fred, 1946-
Sound from a star : a novel / Fred Yager.
p. cm.
Summary: Fifteen-year-old Devon leaves school bullies and his parents'
imminent divorce behind when the person, or being, responsible for
what seems to be music from outer space arrives, with a strange instru-
ment that can be used to heal or to destroy.
ISBN: 978-1-889262-90-1
[1. Music--Fiction. 2. Extraterrestrial beings--Fiction. 3. Healing--Fiction. 4.
Astronomy--Fiction. 5. Family problems--Fiction. 6. Science fiction.]
I. Title.
PZ7.Y1298Sou 2010
[Fic]--dc22   2009044539

Printed in the United States of America

CHAPTER ONE

"I *know you're out there* somewhere," Devon Turner whispered to himself as he watched the stars dance across the western sky. He was searching for a sign. Slowly, he maneuvered a wireless mouse that moved a cursor across a 32-inch flatscreen which, in turn, magically repositioned and focused a Meade Saturn telescope aimed at the western sky. The telescope was connected to a USB port on an Apple computer with a dual processor that allowed him to capture colorful galactic images onto a two-terabyte hard drive.

Devon remembered when he'd first heard the "sound." It was very faint, but it still made him feel all tingly inside, like every cell in his body was laughing. He had tried to describe it to his friend Janice but it was beyond his ability to explain its total effect, so she would just stare at him.

The word *euphoria* didn't quite capture the experience, either. It was something greater, this sound, this vibration, this musical force beyond nature. It was an inter-galactic vibration that had traveled light years to pierce his mind and tonight, by God, he was going to record it for the whole wide world to hear.

Tonight, Devon was in the cat bird seat, looking like the captain of a starship, perched on a high-backed chair in front of his console, a combination super high-speed computer and digital video recorder linked to the strongest telescope civilian money could buy. As he adjusted the scope with one hand, he worked the video capture controls on his state-of-the-art desktop with the other. Turning from the scope, he looked down at the same image illuminated on a three-dimensional liquid crystal display monitor as the computer's processor digitally captured the image of a billion stars through the Saturn's lens and recorded them on one of his two-terabyte hard drives.

At 15, Devon was the youngest student in the junior class at Alpine High School. And while most of his friends were just beginning to drive, or already had their own cars, Devon remain fixated on travel of a higher plane and of much greater distances, ones that spanned the universe, of space and time.

He had converted his bedroom into a mini-planetarium with astronomical charts and maps of galaxies far, far away covering the walls like murals. On the wall over his bed was a constellation map that included a star bearing Devon's name, purchased from the International Star Registry, a birthday gift from his Mom when he turned eleven.

But the room's centerpiece was Devon's complex computer-telescope console, which took up half the space of the room and all of the area in front of the room's only window.

While Devon focused his attention on deep space beyond the Western sky, most residents of the quaint New Jersey community of Alpine cherished their eastern views of the New York City skyline and the George Washington Bridge spanning the Hudson River lit up to look like a giant riverboat.

Devon's bedroom was on the second floor of a white colonial situated between two recently constructed oversized dwellings that he'd heard his father fondly refer to as "McMansions." Devon's house was at the circular end of a tree-lined cul-de-sac, which just so happened to give his bedroom window a perfect view of the western sky.

Once a sleepy bedroom community, Alpine had become one of those upwardly mobile towns where young wealthy homebuyers paid outrageously high prices for what were called "tear-downs" just to have a nice plot of land upon which to build in an up-and-coming community. Devon could barely remember what the area had looked like before developers sold the land on either side of his home.

It was on these two plots that they had built gigantic aircraft carrier-sized homes nearly filling the half-acre upon which they were constructed, leaving scant room for a lawn or any landscaping. This suited the new homeowners just fine since they never spent much time outside. Who needed all those costly lawn maintenance and landscaping fees?

Devon saw something off to the right and shifted the scope so that it pointed at the driveway of the mansion next door. Through the telescope's lens,

Devon watched a father playing basketball with his son under the lights over a three-car garage. The father looked so close that Devon could see the drops of sweat form and fall from the man's face as he took a jump shot. A pang of melancholy echoed around the feelings of emptiness in Devon's chest as he watched with longing something he had never experienced in his lifetime.

Devon's father was an orthopedic surgeon, who rarely spent more than a few waking minutes at home and hardly ever any time with Devon. Therefore, it was at early age when Devon learned how to replace those empty feelings of abandonment and neglect with flights of imagination that took him into other worlds, and where possibilities remained endless.

Sighing deeply, he turned the scope back to the western sky and adjusted the focus while referring to a star map of the galaxies on the wall next to the window. That's when he saw something that didn't seem right.

"I knew it. That star isn't on the map," Devon said, smiling to himself. "I know you're out there. I can feel you. What I don't understand is why someone else hasn't seen you. You'd think that with all this homeland security stuff they'd at least be able to pick up one wandering star, or whatever you're supposed to be. Are you gonna talk to me tonight? Because if you are, I'm ready. So how about giving me something I can work with?"

As Devon worked a joy stick controller that maneuvered the satellite dish on the roof, he noticed the row of withering plants in a dusty corner of the bedroom. A small index card with writing on it read: "The effect of radiation on Himalayan Barley seeds."

How about "the effect of water deprivation on dehydrated plants"—that's more like it, thought Devon. He refocused his attention as he scanned the Western sky with his telescope while re-positioning the satellite dish. Suddenly, a flash of light shot across his lens and the monitor, just as the sounds of muffled voices intruded from outside his bedroom door. As hard as Devon tried to concentrate on the sky, the muffled voices turned into shouts.

"You think you know everything," yelled a male voice, followed by the sound of glass breaking.

"I know I can't live like this anymore!" answered a female voice, as a door slammed closed.

Devon shook his head and then turned back toward the telescope, an expression of sadness and hopelessness on his face. He took in a deep breath, adjusted the focus and forced himself to block out the world that lay just beyond his bedroom door.

"Okay, let's go," pleaded Devon. "Just a little sign, that's all I need," he added, moving the joy stick. On the roof, the satellite dish shifted left and tilted toward the western horizon. Devon looked through the scope and moved the joy stick slightly.

"The kids at school think I'm crazy," said Devon. "They don't believe you exist. So how about a little help, here?"

The satellite dish moved farther left.

Devon sighed and was about to give up. "Maybe they're right. Maybe I *am* nuts." He was moving his finger to the shut down button when the flash of light re-appeared on the horizon. Devon sat up and looked back through the scope.

"That's it!" Devon moved the joy stick to grab the image.

The satellite dish shifted and aimed itself toward the night sky over the western horizon just as it lit up again. This time he could hear a faint but distinctively melodic sound along with the light.

Devon was a young man on a mission as he frantically tried to capture the scene on the western horizon where a cascade of lights shimmered across the sky like the northern lights.

"All right!" shouted Devon. "Yeah baby. That's what I'm talking about!"

CHAPTER TWO

Just *over 25 miles west* southwest of Alpine, New Jersey, down a narrow, two-lane blacktop road, the words printed on the sign chained to a gate read: "U.S. Government. No Trespassing." Next to the gate was a guard shack with an armed sentry on duty. Behind the gate was an even smaller road leading deep into a thick forest where a flash of light filtered through the dense foliage.

The road traveled up a steep hill and into a clearing and an ultra-modern cement building with several antennas and round-shaped communication devices scattered across the roof of the building. Next to the building was a giant satellite dish about the size of a small house. Next to that was a microwave transmitter.

A guard sat at a reception desk reading a Stephen King novel. Behind the guard was a metal door with a small round window. Through the window you could see a long white hallway that seemed to run deep inside the building. Along the hallway were several offices and laboratories where people in white lab coats worked on a variety of experiments. The doors on all but one of these offices were open. There was a sign on the handle of the door that was closed. It was one of those hotel "Do Not Disturb" signs and it looked completely out of place.

One of the lab technicians walked by the closed door, looked at the "Do Not Disturb" sign, and rolled her eyes. She had walked just three steps past the door when an explosion of sound blew the door wide open and then ripped it off its hinges.

The guard at the reception desk dropped the novel as an alarm sounded. He hit some buttons on a console and several television monitors began scanning hallways and offices. Chaos erupted as people ran from the building covering their ears from the booming, piercing sound that blasted from the room where the door had exploded outward.

The guard picked up a phone and started to dial when another door, this one right behind him blew open...and the booming sound blared out. The guard dropped the phone and winced, scrunching up his shoulders and pressing his hands to his ears for protection.

CHAPTER THREE

B*ack in his bedroom*, Devon was frantic. Something was wrong. The red light. Why wasn't it on? He took one last look out the window just in time to see the once-lit horizon go dark.

"Hey! Wait. Don't go yet," he shouted, as he scrambled around the console, checking switches, wondering why the red recording light wasn't on. It was supposed to be on. He hit the record key. Nothing. He got down on his knees and looked under the computer table. Nausea filled his chest.

The light on the power strip where the digital recorder received its power was off. He reached out and hit a switch and the light came on. He must have accidentally turned off the power in all the excitement. The red recording light came back on. He looked back at the window. The sky was dark. "Damn. I'm an idiot. I had it and lost it."

Another sound, this one much closer, caught Devon's attention. It was coming from the hall just outside his bedroom door. It was the sound of footsteps on a hardwood floor. Devon went to the door and opened it just in time to see his father, Arnold Turner, lugging a huge suitcase to the staircase.

"Hey Dad, where ya going? I just got the satellite

dish and telescope hooked up to the computer. You wanta take a look?"

"Ah, not tonight, Dev, I'm in kind of a hurry."

"Come on. It'll only take a second."

"I'm sorry, okay?" pleaded Arnold, a pained look on his face. "It'll be there tomorrow, won't it?"

Yeah, but will you? wondered Devon.

"Yeah, sure, Dad. Tomorrow then."

"I've really gotta run," said his father, picking up his suitcase and carrying it down the stairs. Devon shut the door to his bedroom and let his shoulders sag. A deep sadness rolled over him like a thundercloud darkening a once-bright sky.

Just then Devon saw the tail end of a flash of light fading in the western horizon. "Oh man, you're killing me here. You couldn't wait. They're gonna be so on me at school tomorrow. Maybe I'll stay home sick."

He was about to scan the horizon once more when he heard a knock on his bedroom door. He turned around just as the door opened and his mother, Anita Turner, poked her head inside and looked around the room. She stopped when she came to the dying plants and suddenly she started to cry. Devon got up and went to his mother, putting his arms around her.

"I'm sorry," she said between sobs.

"Don't worry, Mom. He'll come back." Anita sniffled back her tears and blew her nose.

"How are you doin'?" she asked, taking in a deep breath. "You want some supper?"

"Not right now. What's he upset about this

time?" asked Devon.

"He's under a lot of stress. The hospital is cutting back. He may lose his job."

"What's wrong with that? He's always talking about how much he hates his job. How his father made him become a doctor. He could go back to writing songs. That's what he really loves, isn't it?"

"Writing songs won't pay the mortgage."

"So we'll sell the house and rent. We did it before, didn't we? I could get a job after school."

Anita tried to smile but her face crumbled into another sob. She ran out of her son's room.

Devon started to follow her but stopped when he looked at his dying plants. He kneeled down next to the browning leaves and touched one gently. "I know exactly how you feel."

CHAPTER FOUR

A*ll was silent at the* front gate of the compound. In the background, and through the forest, an unearthly blue light filtered through the trees.

The sentry in the guard shack looked dazed as he stared trance-like out at the night.

Inside the white building, sparks were flying everywhere, from the antennas, the transmitter, and the ground. The blue light was everywhere, too, spraying out from the windows.

Bodies lined the hallway like human throw rugs. People in white coats and holding clipboards intermingled with others in civilian dress. Some had their backs propped up against the hallway wall, their eyes open wide and staring out at nothingness. The guard in the reception area sprawled on the floor behind his desk, the paperback he had been reading spread open on the floor nearby. His eyes were open, too, but it was unlikely he could see the shadow that passed behind him or hear the explosive sounds of equipment being smashed.

An unmarked government sedan pulled up to the front gate and two men in off-the-rack "FBI cut" gray suits got out. One held a flashlight aimed through the gate.

"What is this place?" asked the agent who was holding the flashlight.

"Who knows," replied his partner.

"Why are we here?"

"Headquarters picked up some sort of transmission. Briggs said to check it out. We're checkin' it out."

"Transmission? You see any radio towers around here?"

"Come on. Let's get it over with, okay?"

The man not holding the flashlight removed a pair of wire cutters from the trunk and cut open the lock on the gate. He put the cutters back, locked the trunk and joined his partner as they walked to the guard shack, where they found the guard staring into space.

"What the hell?" said the agent, aiming his flashlight's beam. He waved his free hand in front of the unresponsive guard.

"Over there," said the other agent, pointing at the white building at the center of the compound. They began walking toward the building when a light flashed from inside.

"Did you see that?"

"Yeah."

Pulling their government-issued weapons from their hip holsters, they crept slowly toward a window, then stood on either side. They were about to peek in through the window when a blast of sound shattered the window and sent both agents flying through the air. A blue light sprayed through the window over both men who were now lying about thirty feet away and staring up at the sky; their expressions were just like the guard in the gatehouse.

Two hours later, a caravan of Army trucks poured past the gatehouse and through the entrance. The trucks parked in a semi-circle in front of the main building. Soldiers climbed from the trucks and started searching the area. A helicopter flew by overhead as more soldiers entered the nearby woods with rifles and lights. A chopper landed next to the truck caravan and out stepped an army Colonel. His name was John Pemberton and he walked with a swagger as if he owned the place. He had a crooked grin on his face as he surveyed the area. "What the hell happened here?" he asked himself.

One of the soldiers was about to rush by when he stopped and saluted the Colonel who returned the salute. "At ease soldier," he snapped.

"Colonel, Sir. There's someone inside who wants to see you," said the soldier.

"Who would that be?"

Just then a stocky man with short white hair in a gray suit stepped out of the building. "That'd be me, Colonel. Special Agent in Charge, Barton Briggs, FBI."

"What brings you out here, Special Agent...in charge?"

"Two of my men are lying over there staring at the moon. I'd like to know why."

"Agent Briggs, you have any idea what goes on here?"

"No sir, I do not."

"Then let me be the first to inform you that whatever you see or hear at this installation is considered top secret," said the Colonel. "You cleared for that, Special Agent Briggs?"

"Top secret, huh, well whoop dee friggin do. What happened to my men?"

"That's what I'm here to find out," said the Colonel.

"What is this place, anyway?"

"What exactly were your men doing here?"

"Our office picked up a strange transmission coming from this area. I sent them here to check it out. Now I find them in some kind of trance. I'll ask you again, Colonel. What do they do here?"

"I'm afraid if you don't know, I'm not authorized to tell you."

"So much for post 9-11 inter-agency cooperation," snickered Briggs.

In *the forest*, a group of soldiers armed with M-16s and flashlights stopped when one of them spotted something. "Over here." The soldier knelt down as the others joined him. Holding his flashlight with one hand, he put down his weapon and then reached out and picked up an object from the ground.

"Sonofabitch!" he exclaimed as he stared down at the object in his hand. It was a melted, twisted piece of metal that had once been a standard army issue 45 caliber automatic pistol.

About twenty yards away, and hidden in the

trees, someone watched the soldiers search the forest. "*Soldier boys, oh my little soldier boys,*" a male voice sang.

Another convoy of troop transports arrived and parked along the highway leading up to the main gate of the government compound. After one truck emptied, one soldier stayed behind to guard the truck. He looked around and then leaned against a tree. A crackling sound in the woods behind him grabbed his attention as he whirled around, aiming his weapon.

"Who goes there?"

The soldier stepped forward into the woods as something hit a tree. He walked over to where he heard the sound and looked down at a smooth stone. Just then he heard the truck's engine start up.

"Hey!" shouted the soldier as he started running back toward the road. He reached the highway just as the truck that he was supposed to be guarding sped away.

"Come back here!" he shouted, firing his weapon into the air.

CHAPTER FIVE

"*I'm not really sick,*" said Devon into the telephone next to his bed. "I just couldn't face Jason and Mark without proof. But I almost had it. Come on, Janice. You want me to beg? I'm begging you. It's a two-person job."

Janice Perkins held her cell phone away from her frizzy blonde hair and thought for a second, smiled, then nodded. "I'll do it on one condition."

"Okay," said Devon hesitantly.

"You come to the hospital with me when I visit the children's ward."

Devon lowered his head. "Come on. Anything but that. You know how I get around hospitals."

"No. I know what you say. When was the last time you were in a hospital?"

"Ah…15 years ago."

"When you were born? That doesn't count. It's all in your mind, Devon. Just like this sound from outer space. So if you want my help, you'll come with me when I visit the kids with cancer."

"I'll just make them feel worse," pleaded Devon.

"These kids are dying, Devon. They couldn't feel any worse."

"Couldn't I take you to the school dance or something?"

"Ah...I've seen you dance."

"What if I throw up?"

"These kids do that whenever they get chemo."

"Please. Don't make me do this."

"You want my help or not?"

"Okay. Just get over here."

CHAPTER SIX

The Palisades Parkway was filled with mid-afternoon traffic when a lone army truck veered across two lanes to take Exit 4, the Alpine, New Jersey exit, on two wheels.

Downtown Alpine was a contradiction in terms. For one thing, there was not an actual downtown because Alpine wasn't really a town. There was a street with a few commercial establishments, but otherwise the rest of Alpine was entirely residential.

A cable news organization headquartered ten miles away in Teaneck used Alpine whenever it had a story on the "upwardly mobile." So it was not unusual to see a television ENG (which stands for electronic news gathering) truck with a remote microwave transmitter antenna on its roof parked in front of the street's only café.

Inside the café, the ENG crew was catching a late lunch after shooting more B-roll and MOS (man on the street) interviews than the program would ever use.

Preoccupied with their sandwiches, they paid no attention to the Army truck that pulled up just behind the television van until one of the crew members in mid-bite saw their van being driven away.

"Ah, guys. I think somebody just stole our truck."

"Yeah?" answered the field producer. "We still got ten minutes left on our break. Can we get some more coffee over here?" The rest of the crew nodded in agreement. "Rules are rules. Besides, nothing we can do about it now, is there?"

The television van moved slowly down a quiet residential street until it stopped in front of a driveway leading to a ranch style house with a well-trimmed lawn and a red, white and blue sign that read: "For Sale." The television van pulled into the driveway then onto a small patch of lawn next to the garage. It kept moving until it was behind the house and completely out of sight from the street.

Whoever had been driving the van was now somewhere in the rear section moving about and causing the van to rock gently. The sound of movement stopped and the sound of a small motor began to purr as the microwave antenna that had been lying horizontally on the roof was now rising up to a perpendicular position. Once there, the antenna itself began to extend higher until it reached just clear of the roof of the house.

As soon as the antenna attained its full height, the rest of the electronic news gathering van came to life with the sound of switches being thrown, connections made and electronic crackles and pops.

"Ready to transmit signal," said a male voice. "Okay, you lucky devil, whoever you are. Your life is about to change forever."

CHAPTER SEVEN

Devon was on the roof of his house just above his bedroom window adjusting the satellite dish when he yelled down to his open bedroom window, "How's that?"

Sitting inside the window and looking bored, Janice raised her head up from the latest issue of *Wired* magazine and glanced at the LCD monitor. It was filled with digital snow and a hissing sound. "*Nada*," she replied.

On the roof, Devon tilted the satellite dish downward as far as it would tilt until it touched the shingles on the roof. "Now?" he shouted.

The screen still looked fuzzy but an image was slowly forming. "Almost," said Janice.

Janice looked at the box of dying plants in the corner. "Your plants aren't doing very well."

"They're not supposed to do well," said Devon, moving the dish along the roof. "How's it look now?"

Janice turned toward the monitor where a woman was talking in a foreign language. Janice turned up the volume.

"Hey! You got something here."

"Hit record, quick. What is it?"

"Not sure. I think, it might be...yes. A Ukrainian

cooking show, maybe."

On the roof, Devon rolled his eyes and started to tilt the dish down more when he took a step to get better footing. That's when the shingle he was standing on slid loose. Devon quickly shifted his weight to another shingle, but that came loose as well, causing Devon's leg to shoot out from under him. He reached out and grabbed the satellite dish for support. Only his weight was too much and the dish popped out of its stand. Holding on to the dish, Devon began to slide down the side of the roof, grasping at shingles that came loose in his hand as he slid by. He was nearing the edge and was just about to go over when the black cable attached to the dish pulled tight and stopped Devon's fall.

Devon was dangling off the roof with his eyes closed. He reached out with one hand and felt only air.

"Oh boy." He opened one eye and then two and saw that he was dangling outside his bedroom window. The satellite dish itself was stuck on the gutter and pointing straight out over the rooftops of other houses. Devon clutched the cable for dear life and looked into his bedroom window while trying to grab the window sill with his foot. Janice's back was toward him so she didn't even know he was out there.

"Hey! Janice," he shouted. "How about a hand over here?"

Janice continued to stand in front of the LDC monitor with her back to Devon. She seemed to be in a trance.

"Janice!"

A sound was coming from the monitor. It was a familiar sound that started to get louder and louder.

"I can't hold on much longer."

It was then that Devon recognized the sound. "Oh, wow." A smile widened on his face.

Janice was mesmerized in front of the LCD monitor, which showed a swirl of radiant beautiful colors blending in combinations that seemed impossible and not of this Earth. Out of the speakers poured the most beautiful music ever created being played by instruments of unknown origin.

Devon hung outside his window staring at the colors and sound, his body in a state of bliss. Suddenly he snapped out of it and swung through the window and tumbled into the bedroom. He quickly moved to the computer to make sure that this time the red recording light was on and whatever he was seeing and hearing was being recorded. Devon looked at the screen and a wider smile came over his face as he stood transfixed. The colors and sounds were hypnotic.

The music changed and started to sound like a combination of old-time classic rock and roll, remixed into hip-hop with a melody. The music lit up the entire room. Janice and Devon had their mouths open, but were unable to talk. Janice took Devon's hand as they stared enraptured at the screen. They stood there basking in the glow and flow of a mystical vibration. Imagine the sound of light entering your soul and you just might come close to understanding what Devon and Janice were experiencing as they let the sound and vibrations ripple through their bodies lifting their spirits within to a feeling of euphoric harmony with the universe.

All Devon could think of was that tired expression he used to hear, "it just doesn't get any better than this." This, thought Devon, was nirvana—the spiritual place, not the grunge rock band.

Suddenly the transmission ended and the static returned to the screen. Devon and Janice were still in a trance until Devon snapped out of it and turned to the computer. He then hit playback.

Janice slowly returned to a near-state of normalcy as she looked down at herself, at her hands and her arms.

"Can you feel it?" she asked.

"Oh, I feel it all right. Wanta hear it again?

"You recorded it?"

"It's right here."

Devon hit play when Janice grabbed his wrist. "Wait," she pleaded. "Not yet."

Just then Janice noticed something across the room. She walked over to the corner. The once tiny dehydrated plants were now about twice the size they were before and instead of a dying withered brownish color they were now bright green and blooming. Devon walked over and knelt down next to them. He looked back at the monitor and then went to the window and looked out at the bright afternoon sky.

"Okay. You wanta tell me what just happened?" Janice asked, joining him next to the window.

"I'm not sure," admitted Devon.

"Uh, huh. Not sure. I think I'm gonna faint." Janice bent over...then fell back onto Devon's bed, smiling wildly.

"That was *it*, wasn't it? The sound," said Janice, propping herself up on her elbows. "You're right. I do feel like every cell in my body is smiling. That was orgasmic and we weren't even touching."

Janice rolled over onto her stomach and looked at Devon, smiling seductively. "Ah, hah. Now I get it."

"You do?"

"It's some kinda love potion. Devon you little devil."

"What are you talkin about?"

"You just wanted to get me into bed. You are a sly one. It's always the quiet boys."

"Janice. I'm not sure..."

Janice reached out, took Devon's hand and pulled him down onto the bed next to her. She then rolled on top of him and kissed him passionately on the mouth. Startled at first, Devon decided to go along with it until he looked up at the clock on the wall. He quickly pushed her off and stood up.

"The time!"

"Time for love, baby," Janice said, and reached out for him.

"Come on," cried Devon. "We can just about make it."

"Let's make love."

"Janice. Snap out of it." He picked up a water bottle and splashed some water in her face."

"Hey," she complained. "Whoa. What's happening here?"

"We have to move. Come on."

"Where are we going?"

"Manhattan."

CHAPTER EIGHT

A New York City bus stopped at the corner of West 81st Street and Central Park West. The rear door opened and Devon was the first one out, followed by a confused Janice, who stumbled onto the sidewalk and looked around her. She still seemed a little tipsy from the music.

The bus pulled away leaving Devon and Janice facing the American Museum of Natural History. But that wasn't exactly where they were headed. Pulling Janice behind him, Devon walked quickly toward the Hayden Planetarium just behind the museum.

Devon flashed his student ID, and he pulled Janice along down a long hallway to the planetarium auditorium. They entered quietly since a lecture was already in progress. Taking their seats, Devon noticed the audience had its attention turned to the ceiling and the overhead lightshow while the moderator, Professor David Huddleson, a 44-year-old with a Ph.D. in astronomy, with a salt and pepper beard, stood behind a podium and read from his notes.

"Radio and television waves continue on into space indefinitely," said Professor Huddleson as the ceiling played out in mixed media format the astronomer's lecture.

"Say we're on a planet forty light-years away. We'd just now be picking up television signals broadcast forty years ago." As he spoke, the ceiling showed a segment of *Laverne and Shirley*. The audience laughed as they watched the old sit-com.

"I can see those old shows anytime, on Nick at Night," quipped one audience member.

"Okay, how about this old favorite," Professor Huddleson continued. *American Bandstand* came on the ceiling with teenagers from the 1970s with their distinctive haircuts and outmoded dancing. "Can't see this anymore. We'd just be getting a 1970 *American Bandstand* with Dick Clark. Hmm. Maybe this isn't the best example. I mean, Dick Clark. He's still on television today, even after suffering a stroke. The man hasn't aged in forty years. Maybe Dick Clark is an alien."

"Who's Dick Clark?" another student yelled out.

Across the ceiling, more old images danced along: John Wayne in the classic movie western *True Grit* with his horse's reins in his teeth, firing away with both guns blasting; Yul Brenner, wearing a cowboy hat, standing next to Steve McQueen in *The Magnificent Seven*; morphing into Sylvester Stallone as *Rambo*, gunning down a hundred people.

"Think anyone out there is really listening?" asked a man in the audience.

"I think maybe that's why we haven't been contacted yet," said the Professor, nodding at Rambo as he fired off another burst.

"Why?"

"Let me ask you," said Huddleson. "If you saw this guy, would you be in a hurry to come here?"

More laughter as the lights came on to a round of applause.

"Thank you," said Professor Huddleson as he gathered up his notes.

As the crowd poured toward the side exits of the planetarium, Devon and Janice moved quickly to catch up with Professor Huddleson who now had his papers under his arm and was about to slip through a door behind the stage.

"Professor Huddleson," said Devon pulling Janice along with him.

Huddleson turned toward Devon. "Hey, Devon. What are you doing here?"

"You got a minute?"

"Sure. Who's your friend?"

"I'm sorry. Janice, this is Professor Huddleson. Janice is in a couple of my classes."

Huddleson put his papers under his arm and shook Janice's hand. "Pleased to meet you, Janice."

"In your lecture you talk about radio waves going out into space," said Devon, "and what would happen if they were picked up."

Huddleson smiled at Janice. "Devon's only heard my lecture about a dozen times. I think I need some new material."

"What about the opposite effect? Do you think it's possible someone or something out there could send us a signal?"

"Anything's possible."

Huddleson smiled and looked at Janice and then at Devon, who was now holding a blue ray DVD in his hands.

"We'd like you to listen to something."

"What? A broadcast from outer space?"

"Actually," said Devon. "I think that's exactly what it is."

Huddleson smiled quizzically.

"You're serious. What makes you think this came from outer space?"

"It made his dead plants grow," said Janice.

Huddleson looked back at Devon.

"Plus I just recorded this off my satellite dish about an hour ago."

"Let's go to my office," said Huddleson, as he led them down a long hallway.

Professor Huddleson unlocked a door to a cramped office and entered, followed by Devon and Janice. The room was cluttered with mountains of papers, magazines and books piled from the floor almost to the ceiling in every corner. Huddleson cleared away some folders and old manuscripts to reveal a dusty DVD player. He blew the dust away and reached out to accept the disc.

"Don't see many of these any more," said Huddleson. "Why didn't you just download it onto a thumb drive?"

"I didn't have one that could handle what's on here," said Devon.

"Really?" responded Huddleson. "So I still don't know why you think whatever is on here came from outer space."

"I've been tracking something for weeks. A sound, a light, sometimes both. It was always different, but it always appeared on the western horizon in the early evening. Last night I almost captured it but couldn't move my satellite dish fast enough and still work the computer. So today, with Janice's help, I was determined to be ready. I was just trying to shift the direction of my satellite dish when I slipped. The next thing I know, we're seeing and hearing this on my computer." Devon nodded at the DVD.

"Give it to me," said Huddleson as he slipped it into his DVD player, which was connected to an old cathode ray tube television set.

"But this isn't in the early evening," said Huddleson. "You recorded it in the afternoon."

"It's also a lot louder than before, too," said Devon, "and a lot more powerful."

"Real powerful," said Janice.

Huddleson hit play. The television screen came to life as swirling colors filled the screen and the haunting music filled the room. Huddleson blinked and then looked at the colors more closely.

Devon and Janice exchanged a look.

"The speakers," they both said at the same time.

Huddleson appeared as if he was about to go into a trance. Devon turned off the DVD player and Huddleson blinked, then shivered for a second.

"Wow." He smiled at Devon. "I give up, early

Buddy Holly?"

"You think we're crazy, right?"

"Why would I think that? Rock and roll from outer space, huh?"

"You said it was possible."

Huddleson thought for a second, and then removed the DVD from the machine.

"You didn't get the full effect," said Devon. "The speakers on that old television don't really do it justice."

"I don't wanta jump to conclusions, okay? I got a friend at Columbia who knows more about music than anyone alive. He runs the student radio station there. If anyone can figure out where this music came from, he can. Once we've exhausted all the earthly possibilities we can consider the alternatives. Feel like taking a little trip uptown?"

A *taxi pulled up at the* entrance to Columbia University and out stepped Professor Huddleson, Devon and Janice.

"I gotta warn you," said Huddleson as they entered the building housing the music department. "Edgar is a little weird."

Inside, Devon and Janice looked at all the equipment, wall-size amplifiers and speakers, a digital mixing board, and synthesizer. A diminutive man with long white hair sat before the digital mixing board. Edgar French looked like a mad scientist wearing a pair of oversized headphones, flipping switches, twisting dials and dancing in front of a massive console while singing to himself.

"*Do you wanta dance and hold my hand...*" A shadow fell across the mixing board and Edgar turned around. "It's the 'star man,'" he said removing his headphones.

"I was just making some audio files for my man Spider," said Edgar. "You know, the DJ over at QRQ."

"My friends have something you should hear," said Huddleson as Devon handed Edgar the DVD. Edgar smelled it, and Devon exchanged a curious glance with Huddleson. Edgar threw some switches and then turned up the volume.

"You might not wanta make it too loud," suggested Devon. Edgar put the DVD into the computer, put on his headphones, and entered a small recording booth. He grinned at his visitors as he hit play.

A sonic boom blasted from the recording booth, slamming Edgar spread-eagled against one of the glass walls. Devon, Janice and Huddleson froze where they stood, mesmerized by the awesome sound filling the room. It was musical yet otherworldly, with a powerful vibration that permeated everything it touched on a molecular level.

An eerie blue glow of light similar to the one at the government installation sprayed through the cracks around the door of the recording booth. A sound rich and crystal clear filled the room—the sound of perfect harmonic pitch. Janice began to rise in a levitated state but grabbed onto Devon and pulled herself back down.

Suddenly, the sound stopped, allowing a trans-fixed Edgar to slide down the glass wall of recording booth. Huddleson turned slowly toward Devon with a warm smile on his face. The door to the recording booth opened and Edgar crawled out. His long white hair now stuck straight out in all directions, making him look like a human snow cone. Janice just looked stoned, her eyes staring off into space.

Edgar slowly rose to his feet. His hair began to fall back into place. "Wow!" he exclaimed. "Has this been released yet?"

"Released?" asked Devon.

"Released. Available, iTunes, Amazon, in the stores. On the air. Out?" said Edgar sarcastically.

"He doesn't understand," said Devon.

Edgar re-inserted the DVD and threw some switches. He stuck several blank CDs into slots and hit record. "If there's one thing I understand, son, it's music. This, dude, is a chartbuster. Who is it?"

"You were supposed to tell us that. What are you doing?" asked Devon as he watched the bank of re-corders make instant duplicate recordings of the sound.

"Just making a couple copies, okay?" smiled Ed-gar.

"Can you make me a copy?" begged Janice.

"Sure baby," snapped Edgar as he slipped in an-other recordable CD. "Oh, Huddleson my man."

"The music. You don't know what it is, do you?" asked Devon.

"Rest assured my friend, if Edgar French doesn't know a particular piece of music, he knows someone who will. Lemme play it for a coupla DJ friends. Something this good, somebody's gotta know who it is."

CHAPTER NINE

The *street lights were on* in Alpine when a bus stopped at the main intersection of town and let Devon and Janice out onto the sidewalk. Devon walked Janice up to the door of a house not far from the corner. Devon had a look of disappointment on his face.

"Stop looking like you flunked all your finals," said Janice. "Didn't you hear what that crazy guy said? Your music could be a hit."

"It's not my music. We just recorded it off my satellite dish, remember?"

Janice looked directly at Devon, smiling a strong sensual smile. She cupped Devon's face in her hands and gave him a passionate kiss on the lips. She then pulled away, leaving Devon wide-eyed.

"I can't remember feeling this happy. Ever," beamed Janice. You made me very happy, Devon. You, and your music."

"It was pretty great wasn't it?" said Devon.

"I better get inside. It's late," said Janice. "Cheer up, Devon. I have a good feeling about this. We could be famous."

"I don't wanta be famous," said Devon.

"We'll go on *60 Minutes* or *Oprah*. Maybe even

The Daily Show. How cool is that?"

"I'm worried, Janice."

"About what?"

"I don't know. I just don't think we know what we're dealing with here," said Devon.

"Ya know. That's your problem, Devon. You worry about everything. Take a breath and just enjoy life for once. Can you do that? And whatever this is, this music, something this good, you found it, Devon. And I helped you."

Janice leaned in and kissed Devon on the cheek and then went into her house, leaving Devon alone on the sidewalk, gazing up at the western sky.

Later that night, in the room at Columbia where Edgar was listening to a MP3 player of Devon's music, a young black man named Spider entered wearing a leather shirt and lots of jewelry. As he got closer to Edgar, he realized that Edgar was stoned out of his mind, with his headphones on, and his eyes popped wide open.

"Edgar baby, you got my music for the night?" Spider glanced at Edgar and began grabbing thumb drives and CDs and stuffing them in his carry-all sack. He then picked up one of the CDs of the music Devon had recorded. It was marked with a giant question mark.

"Hey! Edgar," yelled Spider as he pulled out the cord connecting the headphones to the console. Edgar sat up as if in a shock.

"You need some rest, man," said Spider. "What's

on this CD?"

Edgar stared at the CD with the question mark in Spider's hand.

"Best damn music you'll ever hear," said Edgar as Spider stuck the CD into his backpack.

"Who is it?" asked Spider.

"No idea," said Edgar. "Some kid named Devon dropped it off.

Spider shook his head and headed out the door. "I ain't playin' any more of that freelance crap you tried peddlin."

"Just give it a listen, Spider," said Edgar, smiling as Spider let the door close behind him.

S*pider's broadcast booth* was only a couple of blocks away from Columbia University. He slipped into a chair just as the previous DJ was leaving, bumping fists in the universal greeting. Spider donned a pair of headphones and began sorting through his collection of CDs.

Grabbing the microphone he began to speak. "Hello, night birds. This is Spider, creeping up on you in the wee hours with a pile of sound." He closed his eyes and reached for the stack of CDs. "This music was carefully selected for your enjoyment." Spider fumbled through the stack, knocking CDs on the floor. His hand picked up the CD with the question mark on it.

"You gotta be kidding me," snapped Spider as he opened his eyes. "What the hell," and slipped the CD into a slot. With the other music still playing, he closed his eyes again. "So, if you're out there and want to rap, give us a call. Meanwhile, sit back, relax and listen to this. It's something new. God help me," he whispered as he hit play.

Spider had his eyes closed as the music began to fill the studio with an energizing force and a blue light. Spider's eyes popped open wide as a huge smile spread across his face.

"Edgar baby, what have we here?"

Outside a taxi drove by and the music from Spider's broadcast poured from the taxi's speakers. The driver looked at his radio, smiled and then stopped his taxi in the middle of the street. Nearby, the same music came from the tiny radio on the shelf of a newsstand. The newsstand's operator grinned foolishly, staring out at space.

Back in his broadcast booth, Spider was talking into a phone and looking at the switchboard in front of him. Every line was lit up.

"I don't know who it is," said Spider into the phone and hit another button.

"Yeah, well, I'm gonna play it again. And I'm gonna keep playing it until somebody tells me who the dude is."

And that's what Spider did. All night long, he played the same CD over and over again.

The sun was coming up over the East River as Spider pushed another button. Devon's music began again just as a door to the booth opened and three men in suits entered. They didn't look very happy.

Spider had his back to the door so he didn't see them. Spider looked very happy. In fact, he couldn't stop smiling and didn't know why. He was usually a melancholy man, alienated, a true night owl living in the opposite direction with the rest of the world. But here in the presence of this beautiful music, Spider felt at peace. He closed his eyes as the shadows of three figures fell across his desk and console.

Behind him, the three men in suits who had entered the booth with stern looks on their faces were now smiling. One of the men tapped Spider on the shoulder. Spider turned around, a glazed, super-relaxed look on his face. The man in the suit took out his wallet and showed Spider an ID card that read Special Agent Howard Powell. The ID had large lettering on it. The letters were FBI. Next to the photo and ID card was a silver badge. Spider looked at the letters and then smiled up at Agent Powell.

"Nice badge," said Spider.

"Thanks. Nice music. Who is it?" asked Agent Powell.

"Got me. Friend of mine up at Columbia recorded it for me."

"Your friend. He got a name?"

CHAPTER TEN

Edgar French was staggering down the street as if he had spent the night drinking. He stumbled up to a row of brownstones and tried to put a key in the door. He was wearing tiny earphones and listening to an IPod. Edgar gave up with the keys and hit the buzzer. Suddenly the door opened and Agent Powell stepped out, followed by the other three FBI agents. Edgar looked at the agents and grinned. One of the agents removed Edgar's earphones. Edgar's smile disappeared and a frown appeared. "Hey man. Don't do that," said Edgar.

"Could we have a moment of your time, Mr. French?" asked Agent Powell.

Devon checked on his once dying plants. They had grown even more since being resurrected by the music he recorded the day before. Dressed for school, he left his bedroom and found his mother in the kitchen leaning against the sink, crying.

"You okay, Mom?"

"Sure. How about some breakfast?"

"I'm already late for school."

Devon kissed his Mother's cheek and touched a

line of a tear on her face. "Dad can be a real ass sometimes, but he'll be back."

"Maybe I don't want him back," said Anita Turner.

"Yeah, but if that's how you really felt, you wouldn't be crying," said Devon, putting his arms around his mother. "He's a bastard."

"Don't talk that way about your father, Devon. He's in more pain than all of us."

"Could've fooled me."

"He is, though, Devon. When your father stopped writing his music, a part of him died, along with his dreams. Whatever you do, Devon, never let go of your dreams. You'd better get to school."

Students and teachers arrived for another day of classes at Alpine High School, battling for position in crowded hallways as they all tried to get to their first period. Along the way, there was the standard amount of horseplay among students rambunctious and full of mischief first thing in the morning.

Devon was stuffing his extra books into his locker when a group of boys surrounded him. The tallest and toughest of the boys, a senior named Jason, pretended to trip and slammed into Devon's locker door, ramming it shut and nearly mashing Devon's hand. Devon pulled it away just in time.

"Hey Turner. See any UFOs lately?" joked Jason as another boy, Shep, tried to grab Devon's books.

"I thought I saw a UFO once," said Shep. "Yeah. It was the pass you dropped against Bergen."

Jason playfully punched Shep in the arm and dragged him away. "Give us a call when the Martians land, will ya Dev?"

Janice arrived just in time to hear the last remark. Devon locked his locker and started walking down the hall with Janice next to him.

"Whatta ya expect?" asked Janice. "You write an article for the school paper about how you're going to make contact with an alien world. People are gonna pick on ya. I told you not to write it, didn't I?"

"What about last night?" asked Devon.

"What about it? You're not gonna write another article, are ya?"

They walked toward a classroom as the first period buzzer sounded.

"Why not? How could you even doubt me now—after what you experienced yesterday? You still don't wanta believe it," asked Devon, sounding more than a little annoyed.

"Believe what?" asked Janice. "That you picked up music from outer space? You recorded some great music off your satellite dish. It probably came from France or some new MTV channel. But outer space? Let go of this alien stuff, okay? It's a little geeky, know what I mean?"

"What about the plants?" said Devon.

"The plants. Okay, you got me there. Look, you don't need dickheads like Jason and Shep laughing at you all the time, okay? I worry about you, Devon."

"Then how about a little support?"

A shadow fell over Devon as a teacher came to the door of the classroom. "Will you be joining us today, Mr. Turner?" asked the teacher.

Janice smiled at the teacher and walked away as Devon let out a sigh and entered the classroom.

Outside, an unmarked government sedan pulled up in front of the main entrance to Alpine High School. Agents Powell and Duggin sat inside looking at the high school.

"A high school kid?" asked Duggin.

"Hey. It was a high school kid who made an a-bomb for his sophomore science project, remember? Half the Third World was ready to hire him," answered Powell.

"So whatta we do now?" asked Duggin.

"We wait. Briggs wants surveillance. Get comfortable. School just started."

Six hours later Janice was running down a hallway as fast as she could. She found Devon at his locker.

"Did you hear it?" she squealed.

"Hear what?"

"Your music, it's everywhere."

"Whatta ya talkin' about?"

"It must have happened sometime between lunch period and study hall. Look. Notice anything different?"

Devon turned and looked around the hallway. Several students were wearing MP3 players, swaying to music. They were all smiling and looking contented.

"Everyone's downloaded your music."

A look of alarm crossed Devon's face as he remembered Edgar French. He looked at Janice. "Guess I wasn't the only one who recorded it."

Jason and Shep closed in on Devon who looked at them with an expression of dread. Jason had a scowl on his face which suddenly became a wide smile. Jason was wearing tiny ear phones attached to an MP3 player. So was Shep who looked equally benign. Devon looked at Jason cautiously.

"Hey. Dev buddy, what do you think of this music?"

"Pretty good. Who is it?"

"Pretty good! Pretty good! You hear this guy?"

"Nobody knows who it is," said Shep, "or where it came from. Whatta gimmick."

"This is the Number One single in the country and nobody knows who he is," added Jason.

Devon grabbed his books and ran outside with Janice trailing behind him. "I have to go see Professor Huddleson," said Devon.

As he and Janice ran off down the street, Agent Powell nudged his partner, Agent Duggin, who had fallen asleep. "Wake up. There's our boy," he said, nodding toward Devon and Janice. He put the car in gear and followed them as they headed toward the transit stop for buses into New York City.

CHAPTER ELEVEN

Professor Huddleson listened intently to what Devon and Janice had just told him.

"It had to be Edgar. He must have bootlegged the music to every radio station in town," said Huddleson. "Who was that person he was making music for when we arrived? Somebody named Spider?"

"There's a DJ named Spider at QRQ," said Janice. "I listen to him sometimes if I can't sleep."

Devon, Professor Huddleson and Janice were escorted into a private office at radio station QRQ. An entourage of people, all with a dazed, drugged look in their eyes followed them. The entourage was led by a fat, bearded man wearing a Hawaiian shirt, the station owner, Max Planco. In the office, Max sat down next to Devon, looking him up and down.

"Are you from the FCC?" asked Max.

"FCC? I'm 15 years old," pleaded Devon.

"Had a narc in here last week looked about 12," said Max.

"The music you're playing," asked Devon, "where did it come from?"

"I didn't do anything wrong," snapped Max.

"Nobody said you did," added Huddleson.

"I run a straight legit operation here."

"So where did you get the music that's on right now?" asked Devon?

"I'll be honest with ya, kid. I don't know where that music came from," said Max. "All of a sudden onc of our DJs was just playin' it. Now I can't get him to take off. I can't even get him to give up his shift. He usually comes on at around midnight and leaves around 4 a.m."

"Is he still here? Can we talk to him?" asked Devon.

"Still here? His shift ended 12 hours ago and he won't leave. And this music, it's the only thing he plays. Follow me."

Max led Devon and the others to a glass-enclosed sound booth where Spider was barricaded inside with files and a chair blocking the door. Max rapped on the door.

"Spider. Hey! Spider," yelled Max, pounding harder. "Somebody wants to talk to you."

"Hear that, people?" said Spider into the microphone. "Is that the sound of opportunity knocking? Not likely. Who could it be?"

Spider turned to the glass wall and looked out at Max and Devon.

"There's a kid out here who claims the music you're playing is his," said Max.

"It's not my music," said Devon. "I just recorded it."

"Right, kid. Let him in, Spider."

"If this is a trick, Max, I'll blow the station. I'll

push up those pots so high there'll be another black-out."

Spider looked at Devon closely. He unlocked the door to let Devon in, then quickly locked it behind him.

"Is this really your music, kid?" asked Spider.

"How'd you get a copy?" asked Devon.

"What's it to ya?"

"Did Edgar French give it to you?"

"You know Edgar?"

"I sorta gave him the music, or he copied it before I could stop him. He was supposed to help us figure out where it came from."

Spider directed Devon to a chair next to his and sat him down.

"So this music is yours?" asked Spider. "Cool. You got any more cuts?"

"No."

"Okay. But you gotta do an album? Don't wanta be no one-hit wonder. What's your name, anyway?"

Devon looked around the studio, which Spider had turned into a bunker, then turned back toward Huddleson and Janice who stood on the outside of the glass-enclosed studio. He felt like a fly trapped in a web as Spider grabbed him by the shirt sleeve and pulled him closer to the microphone.

"Hey! Hey! Hey!" yelled Spider into a hanging microphone. "Have I got a treat for all you good people out there. Right here in Spider's studio. A live interview with the dude who made the music you've been listening to."

Devon put his hand over the microphone. "I

didn't make it. I just—"

"What's your name kid?"

"Ah...Devon. But I didn't create this music. I just recorded it."

Meanwhile, the actual source of the sound was listening intently to Spider's broadcast from inside the television station's stolen ENG van and singing an old George Harrison song: "*If you don't know where you're going, any road will take you there.* —Ah Devon, I bet you're wondering where all this is going."

From a speaker inside the van came Spider's voice.

"Devon. You gotta tell me how you make them sounds, man," said Spider.

Back in the studio, Devon gave Huddleson a "please help me" look. But Huddleson just shrugged back, helpless.

"I never heard nuthin' like that," continued Spider. "What kinda instrument you use?"

"I told you. It's not my music," said Devon.

Spider stared at Devon real hard. "Whatta ya mean, kid?" asked Spider.

"You haven't even been listening to me. I just recorded it off a satellite dish," admitted Devon.

"A satellite dish? Like for television?"

"That's what I've been trying to tell you. I adjusted the satellite dish on our roof to the western horizon. You see that's where I first saw the flash of light. The sound came later. Then yesterday, it came in so clear, like it was just down the street or something. But this music. I think it came from outer space. It's extraterrestrial. I've been tracking it for about a month."

"Whatta ya sayin' kid? ET made this music? Some kinda alien rocker? This is Spider you're talking to. Don't you be runnin' no scam on me."

"I'm not scamming you, Spider. This music, it made my dying plants grow," said Devon.

Spider stared at Devon. "Your plants?"

"They were dying. It was for a stupid science project to show the harmful effects of radiation on plant life. Only after I downloaded this music, they were blossoming again."

Spider wrinkled his brow. "Wait. You're sayin' this is music from some alien and this music brought your dead plants back to life, or something like that?"

"Something like that," said Devon. "But mostly, what I'm trying to say is that I think this music is from outer space."

In *the stolen TV van*, a hand wearing a strange-looking glove turned up the volume to hear Devon's answer. "Oh Devon, baby, you just made my day," said a male voice.

"You folks hearin' this out there?" came Spider's voice over a speaker in the van.

"Oh yeah," said the male voice. "We're hearing it.

Oh boy are we hearing it. Music from space, huh? Sounds good to me."

Back in the studio Spider was pacing around his domain like a caged animal. He looked at Devon, shaking his head. "This is special, man," said Spider. "Outer space? What do we call it? 'Sound from a Star.' All right. Does the Spider make it happen or what? Whatta ya say, kid? Think this dude'll come down and put on a concert?"

Devon looked out to Huddleson and Janice again for help but they just stared back.

"Wouldn't that be something, huh?" asked Spider. "A concert. The first Alien concert. Whatta you people say out there? You people want a concert? Give me a call."

Every phone line lit up.

CHAPTER TWELVE

Devon, *Janice and Huddleson* left the radio station building and started to walk back to the street when Devon stopped and looked around.

Something had changed. Traffic wasn't moving even though the lights were green. People were walking down sidewalks but in a meandering, trance-like way. That was when he heard it. Faint at first, coming from a window of one of the cars stopped at a green light. The sound. His sound. People wearing little white ear phones, or were listening on car radios. He could hear it from nearby apartments where the windows were open. The sound Devon had recorded off his satellite dish was filling the air around Times Square, replacing the normal buzz of car horns and traffic.

As they walked past a barber shop, Devon studied the barber who was holding an electric shaver and shaving his customer's head. But neither he nor the customer seemed to care. Both had dazed expressions of euphoria on their faces as the barber shaved the man bald. The man in the chair losing his hair didn't seem to mind as they listened to the "music" coming from a large radio on a counter behind the barber's chair.

Huddleson smiled at Devon. But the look on Devon's face revealed more than a little apprehension. "It's like a drug," said Devon. "Look at them. What are we gonna do?"

"Do?" replied Huddleson. "Enjoy it kid, while it's still legal."

The music had filled the air. Every radio station and MTV channel in the city was playing the music Devon recorded off his satellite dish. People sat at computers downloading bootleg copies into their MP-3 players. Music stores were burning CDs as fast as they could and selling them on the spot as fast as they could make them. Street hawkers started selling bootleg CDs on the corner with their bootleg DVDs.

As Devon, Janice and Huddleson wandered along Broadway, they saw a newscaster and cameraman with a copy of the latest *Daily Variety*.

"For the first time in recording history a bootleg tape of music by an unknown artist is at the top of every music chart," said the newscaster outside Tower Records. "The music everyone is calling 'Sound from a Star' is virtually the only thing radio stations even play anymore."

He held up a copy of *Billboard* magazine and pointed to the "Top 100 records" with a "?" at Number One.

Devon let out a deep sigh. "I better get home."

"You're a star now, Devon," said Huddleson. "You have to take precautions."

"Whatta ya mean?"

"Your life is no longer your own. You're a celebrity and that means the public thinks they own you."

"But I don't want to be a celebrity," said Devon.

"You should have thought of that before exposing the world to your music."

"But it's not my music. I just recorded it."

"Right. Well, I doubt that's gonna make much of a difference. But hey, I'm just an astronomy professor. What do I know?"

"And I have a trigonometry quiz the first period tomorrow so I better get home," said Devon.

As Devon and Janice walked toward the Port Authority Bus Terminal, an unmarked government sedan followed slowly behind.

"This is bad," said Agent Powell as he looked out the window of the sedan at all the people walking around 42nd Street like zombies. He turned to the other agent who had a goofy smile on his face and his head pressed against the passenger window.

"Oh no," said Powell, shaking the other agent. "You took out your ear plugs. Briggs is gonna be pissed."

CHAPTER THIRTEEN

Devon *had tossed and* turned all night, worry bouncing around his brain like a ping pong ball between what to do about the music, and about all those trigonometry theorems he had tried to memorize before drifting off about midnight.

By the time he reached school on his bike, he was ready to go back to sleep. He looked at his watch and saw he had five minutes to park and lock his bike and make it to trigonometry class. He rolled up to the metal bike rack and was about to get off when a group of reporters and television mini-cam operators surrounded him.

Devon clicked his Kryptonite bike lock into place and tried to push through the crowd that had encircled him.

"Excuse me," said one rather pushy female reporter, sticking a microphone in his face. "Are you Devon Turner?"

"No, now get out of my way. I'm late for class," snapped Devon.

Just then Jason and Shep walked by smiling.

"Hey, Dev!"

"Morning, Devon."

"Busted." The pushy newscaster smiled at him.

"We understand you have something to do with the sound that's taken over the airwaves," she said. "Wanta tell me about it? Have you been in contact with the extraterrestrial responsible?"

"What?" Devon pushed past the newscaster only to be blocked by another reporter and cameraman.

"There's a rumor going around about a concert? Any truth to that?"

"Concert!" shouted Devon. "Who are you people?" He pushed his way past another throng and entered the school lobby closing the doors behind him. As he walked to his locker a thought began to form and when he finally reached it he opened his mouth and said aloud. "A concert. Why not a concert?" As Devon started to open his locker he sensed something behind him and spun around.

Standing in a semi-circle around Devon were six of the school's most beautiful girls.

"Morning Devon," they all said in unison. Then one broke away from the group and sidled up against him. "Doing anything tonight, Devon?" she asked. "Here's my number. Call me. Any time."

"Me too," said another as they walked off fluttering their eyes, leaving Devon dumbfounded.

Devon stared down at the piece of paper with the phone number when Janice appeared in front of him, reached out and snatched the note from his hand. Before he could utter a sound she tore the note into tiny pieces and stormed off.

Throughout the rest of the day, wherever Devon went, students who had never acknowledged his existence before were waving and smiling at him. Girls would flirt. Boys would pat him on the back and say, "Way to go." It was the first day in a long time that Devon could remember that school didn't suck—in spite of his trigonometry test.

As he climbed on his bike at the end of the day he almost felt sad that it was over because he doubted he'd ever experience another day like that ever again. Devon pushed away and began to peddle home, completely oblivious to the unmarked dark gray government sedan that had pulled away from a curb right behind him.

Janice, on the other hand, had seen everything. Frustrated that Devon had left school without her, she stood at the foot of the school steps and watched the car as it crept along behind him. "Devon!" she shouted, but he was too far away to hear. She watched as he turned a corner with the sedan right behind him.

"They could be kidnappers," said Janice aloud. "Oh my God! I gotta warn him."

CHAPTER FOURTEEN

As soon as *Devon entered* his home, his mother handed him the phone. "It's for you. It won't stop ringing," she said.

Devon put the phone to his ear. "Hello."

"Dev baby. It's Spider here. Your favorite DJ. Hey man. You gotta get us some new sounds. This is great stuff but it's kinda like drinking recycled soda. My listeners are getting restless. You gotta respect the public. Hear what I'm saying?"

"I hear you but I don't have anything else," said Devon.

"N-G. N-G."

"N-G?" asked Devon.

"No good. You better get some new tunes. No telling what's gonna happen. They crave your stuff. It's an addiction. They need it. Don't let us down Dev baby. We're counting on you. A new fix. Just like the old fix, but new. New tunes baby. Gotta run." Click!

Devon looked at the phone and set it down. New tunes? How was he going to get new tunes? They weren't even tunes to begin with, just sound waves from space.

"Any homework?" asked Anita.

"No," said Devon. "I've gotta do something, Mom." And with that he rushed up the stairs to his room and closed the door. Dropping his book bag on the floor, Devon sat down at his console and immediately began moving the joy stick and scanning the sky. "Please be out there."

Suddenly the phone rang and Devon lifted it from its charger.

"Now what?" he asked impatiently.

"Are you all right?" asked Janice.

"No, I'm not all right. This thing has gotten out of hand."

"Want me to come over?" she asked.

"I think I'd like to be alone for awhile," said Devon.

"Somebody followed you home," said Janice.

"What?"

"I saw a dark gray car. It followed you when you left school. Somebody might be trying to kidnap you. Hold you for ransom because your music is so popular."

Devon went to his bedroom window and looked outside. A dark gray car was parked at the foot of the driveway.

"They're outside," said Devon. "I gotta go." Devon hung up the phone then went to his computer console. He turned it on and gazed at the blank screen. "How am I supposed to get in touch with you?"

Just then the screen became a swirl of mesmerizing colors. Devon stared, transfixed. The speakers on the side of the monitor began to crackle and pop.

And then came a voice.

"Devon?"

Devon peered at the screen. "Yeah?"

"We caused quite a stir, didn't we?" said the voice. Devon's mouth dropped open as he stared at the screen, wide-eyed.

"I figured it's time we had a little talk, but it looks like you're gonna have some visitors, so I'll be brief," continued the voice.

Devon moved closer to the screen. "Visitors?" asked Devon. "What visitors?"

"Get your hands on a microwave transmitter. Frequency J," the voice commanded.

"Who are you?" asked Devon.

"Otherwise you'll just be talking to your TV screen. Aim the microwave in the same direction your dish is pointing. I'll wait for your call."

The screen went blank and the voice was replaced with a hissing sound. Meanwhile, outside, a dozen government sedans pulled into Devon's driveway. Men in suits climbed out of each car headed for the front door and rear of the house. Among them were the FBI men who'd spoken to Edgar and Spider, only now they weren't smiling.

Agent Powell, along with Agent Duggin, led one group to the front door. Agent Powell knocked.

Anita Turner opened the door and her smile immediately turned into a look of concern.

"Can I help you?" she asked.

"Sorry to bother you, ma'am," said Agent Powell as he flashed his FBI badge. "We'd like to see your son."

"Devon? What has he done?"

"We'd just like to talk to him."

"I don't understand," said Anita. "What's going on?"

"That's strictly a need-to-know, ma'am."

"Well I'm his mother so I need to know before I'll let you in this house. How strict is that?"

Devon *was still staring* at the television when he heard a knock on the door.

"Devon?" said Anita. "Open the door, please. Some people are here to see you."

Devon got up, walked to the door, unlocked it and pulled it open. The hallway was filled with men in suits standing behind his mother.

"Mom?" asked Devon.

"This is the FBI, Devon. They have a few questions."

Devon shook his head as Agent Powell entered his room and looked around. He walked over to the computer console and examined the telescope attachment.

"Devon Turner, would you please come with us?" asked Agent Powell in the gentlest FBI voice he could muster.

"Am I being arrested?" asked Devon.

"No, son. We just need to ask you some questions and we prefer to do so in a neutral location."

"How neutral?"

✦

T*he room was undersized* and sparsely furnished with a table and four chairs. An old television set was mounted on the wall. The so-called neutral location turned out to be the FBI field office in Teaneck, New Jersey. Devon sat at the table with his mother and two agents, including Agent Powell, who led the interrogation.

Flipping on a tape recorder, Agent Powell began. "The music, son, where'd you get it?"

"I recorded it off a satellite dish," said Devon.

"Who sent it to you?"

"Sent it to me? Nobody sent it to me. I found the signal and recorded it."

"Then why were you the only one who received it?"

"I don't know."

"Who are you working with?" asked Agent Powell.

"Working with? Well, my friend Janice helped a little, and then I took the music to Professor Huddleson. But he didn't know who could have created it, so we visited a friend of his, Edgar French."

Agent Powell nodded. "We already spoke with Mr. French. Do you know if Professor Huddleson has ties to any terrorist organizations?"

"He's an astronomer."

Just then the door opened and Chief Agent Briggs entered.

"What the hell's taking so long?" demanded Briggs. "You know what's goin' on out there?"

"Out where?" asked Devon.

"Son, that music you pulled down is causing us a

major headache. The Country's goin' down the toilet. Nobody wants to work anymore. Your music is having a detrimental effect on the nation's productivity," snarled Briggs. "Turn on the TV."

One of the agents hit the "on" button of the television and on the screen came images of workers walking around listening to music instead of working, factories shutting down, secretaries and their bosses dancing to the music. "Everybody's goin' whacko," continued Briggs. "Half-built cars are piling up on assembly lines, unfinished. Nothin's gettin done."

Devon looked at the television and saw a trading floor where the traders were just sitting back listening to the music instead of buying and selling stocks.

"So I just got one question for you, son," said Briggs as he stood face to face with Devon. "Who's behind it? The Chinese? Al Qaeda? The French?"

"The French? Look. All I know is that I recorded it off my satellite dish."

Briggs slammed his hand down on the table and began pacing the room.

"You might have some folks fooled with this music from space crap," said Briggs. "But I don't buy it—understand? 'Sound from a star,' my ass. This country's got a lot of enemies and they'd like nothing better than to see us in a state of economic weakness. Hell, we just came out of the worst recession since the Great Depression. We're already in one big money war. The dollar ain't worth crap anymore. And this music was just a trick to get everyone to stop working. Well guess what? It didn't work. We shut down the radio stations and confiscated their tapes. As of now, the music is banned from the airwaves. I've got my eyes on you, boy. Now get him outta here."

CHAPTER FIFTEEN

*A*gent *Powell stopped the* unmarked government sedan in Devon's driveway to let Devon and his mother out. They were about to head for the front door when out of the bushes stepped a man wearing a bright green blazer and plaid pants.

"Get back. I've got mace," shouted Anita.

"Please ma'am. I'm not here to hurt you. In fact, I may be able to make you both very rich."

"Not interested. Come on Devon," said Anita and she started to push Devon toward their house.

"Devon. You're gonna wanta hear what I have to say."

Anita turned around and stepped up to the man. "And why is that?"

"Because I'm the man who's going to save your life."

"Are you threatening my son?"

"No, ma'am."

"Who are you?"

"The name's Smythe, and that sounds like tithe. I'm a ten percenter. A promoter by trade. I book all the top acts. From the Stones to Usher. Miley Cyrus to Madonna. Brittany, Whitney and Pitney."

"Who's Pitney," asked Devon.

"Never mind. Before your time. But you, my friend, are going to be the biggest act I ever booked. In fact, I've already sold out the Meadowlands. Tomorrow night. It's the only place available and it's the only way to satisfy your fans. They're ready to kill for that music of yours. Now that the radios have stopped playing it they're craving it even more. You let 'em down, they'll tear you apart."

"Then I'm dead already," said Devon. "Goodnight, Mr. Smythe."

Devon started toward his house.

"You can't put the genie back in the bottle."

"What's that supposed to mean?"

"You don't show up at the Meadowlands tomorrow night, you can just kiss your ass goodbye."

With that, Smythe tipped his forehead with his hand and melted back into the shadows.

As soon as Devon got inside he called Professor Huddleson. "I need a microtransmitter."

B*ecause it was pitch-black* behind Devon's house, Huddleson didn't see the garbage can that some enterprising night animal had tipped over. He almost tripped, nearly dropping his end of the long ladder he and Devon were carrying. Janice was right behind them holding a large microwave transmitter with a transponder in its center for sending a signal skyward.

"What if he won't do it?" asked Devon struggling with Huddleson to lift the aluminum ladder and set it against the side of Devon's house. The tip of the ladder barely reached the edge of the roof.

Huddleson in turn handed the antenna to Devon. "It's your party, pal. He told you to get a microwave transmitter and we got a transmitter. I'll hold the ladder."

Devon gripped the microwave antenna in one hand and began climbing toward the roof.

Once there, Huddleson and Janice went inside to Devon's bedroom to set up the computer console and telescope. Janice opened a window and leaned out to watch Devon use a battery-powered drill to screw the microwave in place next to the satellite dish. Huddleson checked the settings on the computer to make sure the dish and microwave were aimed in the same direction.

"All set!" shouted Huddleson.

Devon lowered himself into his bedroom through the window and sat down in front of a microphone. He turned to Huddleson. "What do I say?"

"'Hello' always works for me."

The sound of Anita Turner's voice from downstairs interrupted them.

"Devon? You and your friends need a snack or anything?"

"No, thanks, Mom!" Devon called back. He listened for her footsteps, but she remained quietly downstairs.

Devon raised his eyebrows at Professor Huddleson, then turned back to the mike.

"Ahem. Ah. Hello out there," said Devon. "Can you hear me? This is Devon Turner calling."

Janice looked out the window at the satellite dish

and microwave. A red light on the microwave blinked whenever Devon talked. In the distance the stars were twinkling out their own galactic rhythm.

"Remember," said Devon. "You said to call." He waited for a response but nothing came through the speakers except a low hissing sound. Devon looked at Janice and Huddleson, who nodded for him to continue.

"It's not working," said Devon.

"Give it time," urged Huddleson. "Just keep talking."

"Are you there? Hey. We have to talk," continued Devon. "Things have gotten outta hand. Your music, it's gotten too popular. You have to put on a concert. —Oh man. How could you know what a concert is? I'm dead. Forget it."

Devon started to get up when the TV monitor shifted from snow and static to a blue white light.

"A concert?" said a male voice.

Devon looked at Huddleson, wide-eyed. "You're there."

"Who's there with you? The FBI?" asked the voice.

Devon didn't know it but Agent Powell and another agent were indeed listening to the conversation from a car down the street.

Devon looked around the room and then back to the microphone. "I'm just here with some friends. The FBI isn't here."

"They're there. You just can't see them."

Agent Powell rolled his eyes.

Devon looked around his room again and

shrugged. "Who are you?"

Silence.

Devon stared at the silent speakers. "You don't have to tell me if you don't want to. It's just easier to..."

"What's this concert you were talking about?" said the voice. While neither Devon nor the FBI could see it, the voice was coming from the van still parked behind the vacant house a few blocks away.

"Tomorrow night," said Devon. "This crazy promoter booked the Meadowlands for a concert expecting us to just show up. Of course, we know..."

"What time?"

"Time? Ah...eight?"

"Let me check my schedule."

Devon shook his head. Huddleson and Janice both smiled.

"I think I can make it," said the voice.

"You can? That's great."

"Tomorrow, then." The television monitor went to snow and static.

"Hey! Wait!"

In *the unmarked government* car near Devon's house Powell turned to the other agent and said, "Call Briggs."

D*evon stared at Huddleson* and Janice with a look of bewilderment on his face. "What have we done?"

"Guess we'll find out tomorrow night," said

Huddleson. "Hey, I gotta get that transmitter back to the city. Do you mind?"

But Devon was too dumbstruck to even move. "Forget it," said Huddleson. "I'll do it. See you to-morrow."

Huddleson climbed out the window and up on the roof as Janice walked over to Devon and looked at him shyly. "You did it."

"Did what?" said Devon. "We don't know what we're doing or what we're dealing with and I just invited it to come down and put on a concert."

"Okay, so it's a little risky. ET was kinda cute."

"Yeah, but what if it's not ET? What if it's more like the Predator? Or that thing that comes out of people's chests—Alien? Why did he pick me?"

A *few blocks away*, the TV van that was still parked behind the vacant house was now rocking back and forth and a faint but familiar sound was seeping through a hairline crack in a rear window. It sounded as if someone was moving back and forth, possibly practicing and playing different melodies on an unknown instrument. "The Meadowlands," the voice cried out. "Oooo Mamma. If only you could see me now. Your baby boy's gonna be a rock star."

CHAPTER SIXTEEN

Devon *was sitting on* his bed pondering his fate when Janice looked at her watch. "Oh boy, we're gonna be late," she said reaching out and pulling Devon to his feet. "Come on."

"Late for what?"

"The hospital," said Janice. "Remember our deal? I helped you and now it's your turn to help me. It's volunteer night at the children's ward."

"Oh no," said Devon. "I can't do that."

"You promised," Janice insisted, practically dragging Devon down a hallway and toward the front door.

"I can't," said Devon.

"Sure you can," said Janice. "These kids are dying, Devon. Let's see if we can bring a little joy into their lives."

A *bus dropped them* off at the hospital's main entrance. Janice walked to the front entrance, pulling Devon behind her. She opened the door and pushed Devon inside.

The children's cancer ward was on the fifth floor and all the way up in the elevator Devon tried to think of one more excuse that would satisfy Janice. But nothing came to him. How could he tell her that hospitals gave him nightmares? That it wasn't the children—it was the location. Whenever his father was operating, he dreamed that the patient was him and his father was cutting him open, pulling out organs and entrails. He thought he was going to vomit when the elevator doors opened and Janice pushed him into a room full of bald children.

The children stopped what they were doing and turned toward Devon and Janice. Devon had a look of sheer terror on his face. A little boy walked over to him and looked up.

"You gonna chuck?"

Devon tried to smile at the child, but quickly put his hand over his mouth and rushed for a restroom.

Janice let out a deep sigh and grinned at the boy. "Hey, wanta play checkers?"

"What's the matter with your friend? The chemo getting to him?"

"Something like that," said Janice. "He'll be okay. It's his first time."

At *FBI headquarters in* Teaneck, a group of men in suits were listening to Chief Briggs. "I don't know what's going to happen tomorrow night, but I want us to be prepared for any contingency. I don't care if he's a Martian, a terrorist, or Bruce Springsteen's cousin. He, she or it shows up at this so-called concert, we terminate.

"I know what you're thinking. What if it really is

an alien? What about our humanity and for the good of science and all that? According to the top scientists at every institution in the land, this music is highly addictive to better'n 90 percent of the general population, and, well, let me remind you that if we continue on the course we're going, we won't have a country. And if we don't have a country, we don't have to worry about humanity or science because there won't be any of that, either."

Briggs walked among the agents as he talked.

"Did any of you see today's paper?" He paused and the agents just looked at each other. "Did you? No. Of course you didn't. There wasn't a paper today. Nobody's working. They're all listening to that damn music. God I hate that music."

CHAPTER SEVENTEEN

A mammoth stage was constructed in the center of Byrne Arena at the Meadowlands of New Jersey. Workmen were still setting up giant speakers that looked like undersized apartment buildings. Edgar French was there directing the sound crew. On the stage, Mr. Smythe paced back and forth. Thousands of people were pouring into the stadium from a parking lot filled with cars. A television news helicopter flew overhead. Excitement was in the air.

Devon and Janice arrived and joined Smythe and Huddleson on the stage.

"Music! Music! Music!" chanted the ever-growing crowd.

"It's about time, kid," said Smythe, walking over to greet Devon. "Didn't think you were gonna show."

Smythe walked out onto the stage wearing his gold sportscoat, his trademark, and the audience went wild. "How you all doin' tonight?" he asked.

The crowd cheered as Smythe walked from one side of the stage to the other, talking all the while.

"All right. I got a few announcements to make. This concert is sold out."

Another loud cheer shook the grandstand.

"The New Jersey Turnpike is closed. Traffic is

gridlocked all the way into Manhattan." Smythe looked back at Devon. "You ready?"

Devon's eyes widened. "You don't understand. It's not me. I'm not responsible for the music. But he's gonna show. Or at least he said he was. Maybe he's stuck in traffic."

"Better hope not, kid," said Smythe as he turned back to the audience.

"You people are the chosen, the lucky ones who made it."

FBI Agents Briggs and Powell walked among the crowd, scanning faces, looking around.

"Can you feel the excitement in the air?" asked Smythe.

"Cut the crap," shouted someone from the audience.

"Get to the music!" screamed another.

Smythe turned toward Devon. "I can't stall them any longer."

"He said he'd be here," said Devon.

"Tough luck, kid," said Smythe. He looked around until he spotted a man standing in the shadows. He nodded to him. The man left. The promoter turned to Devon.

"I did what I could. I filled the stadium, packed the seats. It's a shame."

"What do we do?" asked Devon.

"Do?" said Smythe. "That's up to you, kid. Me? I'm outta here. I've seen how ugly these things can get when the act doesn't show up. It's been swell, kid. Good luck." Smythe started to leave the stage.

"Hey! Where are you going?" shouted Devon.

"I warned ya. Didn't I warn ya? Don't screw your fans. You screw your fans and they'll rip out your heart."

Just then a two-person helicopter rose up behind the stage and Smythe climbed aboard. Devon stood with his mouth open as the chopper took off and disappeared behind the nosebleed seats.

Devon turned back toward the crowd which looked like it was ready to storm the stage. Angry faces shouted up at Devon. The police were poised for action. The angry mob started moving closer.

A fist fight broke out in front of the stage. Punches were thrown. One man got nailed in the face. Another was slammed over the head by a folding chair. A third was about to get tossed to the ground when the man holding him looked up and froze.

A lone figure under a spotlight was sliding down a highwire toward the stage from somewhere near the rear top of the stadium. It was if he had come out of nowhere, lit from an unknown source of light. As it got closer, the figure appeared to be holding a strange looking instrument, which he was strumming. Each strum caused light and sound to wash across the stadium like a wave.

The groups of men who were about to come to blows dropped their fighting stances and turned toward the music. Harmonic vibrations entered their hearts and minds as the vibrations smoothed out conflicts the way waves of the sea smoothed the sand on the beach.

On the side of the stage, Briggs and his army of

FBI agents waited in the wings. They were all wearing ear plugs. "You men ready?" shouted Briggs. "Here he comes."

A convoy of Army trucks arrived at the main gate of the stadium and soldiers poured out to guard any escape route. Other soldiers took their places around the perimeter.

Back on stage, FBI Agent Powell pushed in front of Devon and Janice. "Get behind me," he ordered.

"What are you doing?" asked Devon.

Powell cocked the hammer on his pistol just as the "sound" they'd been hearing began to fill the stadium.

Swirling colors, like the unearthly hues on Devon's television monitor, filled the night sky above the stadium like an aurora borealis. Bright beautiful colors, blending like a painter's palette washed across the night sky as music filled the stadium with light and sound.

From the stage, Devon looked out at the crowd which began to divide as a beam of light and sound made a path from the rear of the stadium to the stage. And into this light the lone figure with the strange instrument walked toward the stage. Each time he strummed the instrument, rays of light sprayed out. As the figure moved closer, Devon notice that he bore a striking resemblance to a heavy metal rocker as he walked up to the stage throwing off an array of laser beams and lights.

The crowd screamed when the figure reached behind his back and then swung around, aiming his instrument at the audience. He banged out a series of vibrations and light that knocked a few people on their butts.

Devon saw Agent Powell aim at the figure. Powell put a hand to his ear to hear an order coming over his earpiece. "Powell. You got a clear shot. Take him out." Powell was about to squeeze the trigger when the figure holding the strange instrument whirled around, aimed at Agent Powell, and hit a sour note.

A brutal, ear-ripping, harsh-sounding chord sent a vibration that looked like a lightning bolt right at Powell. The bolt of energy zapped through the air between the instrument and Powell's gun, freezing Powell in his stance.

The gun in Powell's hand began to glow red-hot and started to smolder. Powell cried out in pain as he dropped his weapon on the stage. He looked down at the gun as it slowly turned into liquid melting into the wooden platform. Powell covered his injured hand as the crowd gasped.

Devon looked down at the melting gun and then at the strange looking figure on the stage who was grinning back at Devon.

"I'm here," he said. "And I'm here to play." With that he began strumming harmonic sounds that lit the entire arena in a heavenly glow.

Devon looked around and slowly approached the strange-looking figure. Time seemed to stop. Devon glanced back at Powell and at his melted gun and then turned toward the man with the strange looking instrument. A surge of fear rippled through Devon's body. This can't end well, he thought.

"I'm not gonna bite," said the Stranger, still strumming.

Briggs was about to bark an order when he felt a hand on his shoulder. He turned to see Colonel Pemberton from the government installation.

"We need him alive," said Pemberton.

Devon hesitantly walked closer to the strange figure. "Ah....I'm Devon."

"How do you do, Devon?"

"What....what do I call you?"

"You can call me Gordon."

"Gordon?"

"That's my name. Got any requests?"

Devon looked around just as Huddleson gave him the thumbs-up sign.

"Requests? Ah...just play. Play anything you want," said Devon.

"Well, okay then." And with that he began to play. Only this time, when he strummed the unusual instrument, even more beautiful sounds and vibrations filled the arena. Gordon shifted direction and strummed again. He then began to play a haunting combination of old time rock and roll, rhythm and blues, Buddy Holly, Elvis, the Beatles, as well as some recent Maroon 5, Nickleback, U-2, Bon Jovi, and Madonna, mixed in with some classical music and jazz. A blend of every type of music ever broadcast over the air waves.

In the crowd, the music and vibrations had a strange effect on people. Everyone was smiling at each other. The entire venue took on a new aura. All of the anger and viciousness of a few minutes ago had disappeared, replaced by gentle caring feelings people in the audience began to express toward each other, taking hands, embracing. Then, something even more astonishing occurred.

A bloody cut on the arm of someone in an earlier fight began to heal. A black eye on another fighter started to disappear. Agent Powell looked at his burned hand healing before his eyes. A crippled man looked down at his legs and slowly rose from his wheelchair, his face aglow with joy.

Gordon strummed the instrument into a hallelujah-type crescendo climax while smiling at Devon and Huddleson, causing the entire stadium to take on a halo-like glow. When he finished, a hush fell over the crowd. Then, from the background, voices began to be heard...faint at first but getting louder: *It's a miracle. I can walk. My arm healed. I can see. I can breathe!*

Devon gazed out at the crowd as Gordon took his bows. Gordon looked over at Devon and motioned for him to join him. Devon walked over slowly. Suddenly, a dozen FBI men surrounded the stage with guns drawn. Chief Briggs and Colonel Pemberton stepped forward.

"If he makes a move, shoot him," ordered Briggs.

"Whoa!" said Gordon. "If you didn't like the number just say so."

Devon put himself between Gordon and the FBI men. "No!" he shouted.

"Get outta there, kid!" screamed Briggs.

Devon turned to Gordon. "They think you're trying to destroy the country with your music. They're a little pissed off."

"They're the FBI," answered Gordon. "It's their job to be pissed off."

Just then a man with long hair walked on to the edge of the stage. FBI agents grabbed the man before he got too close. "Hey," yelled the man. "Take it easy."

"Beat it, pal," said Agent Powell.

"See that wheelchair down there?" said the man, pointing. Everyone on the stage looked down into the seating area at an empty wheelchair.

"I've been sitting in that chair since the first Iraq war," said the long-haired man. Agent Powell held the man back as he tried to walk. "This is the first time in fifteen years that I've been on my feet. *He* did it. His music healed me," said the man, pointing at Gordon.

Powell let the man go free and he walked over to Gordon and shook his hand. "Thanks, dude."

The crowed cheered wildly.

"You liked the number?" said Gordon. "It wasn't too eclectic?"

"Liked it?" said the long-haired man. "You healed my leg, man."

"I know, but what about the song? Did it work?"

The man stared at Gordon and then smiled, "You're too much, man."

The long-haired man leapt off the stage and into the crowd, who caught him and then started to chant, "More! More!"

"They like me," said Gordon, beaming. He strummed the instrument, and the rift lit up the entire stage. He aimed his instrument at the lights on the top of the stadium and hit a power-chord that sent a jolt straight at the light, causing it to explode into a rainbow of colors. The crowd looked stoned as it swayed to the music, caught in its haunting melody, as if at one with the vibrations.

Briggs scratched his head and leaned in close to the Colonel, nodding toward Gordon warily.

"A healer, huh? Look at those people out there. You call that healing?"

"They look pretty happy," said Colonel Pemberton.

"They're stoned-out zombies," said Briggs. He then walked over to Gordon who flinched when he realized Briggs was so close. Briggs stared at the instrument and then abruptly tried to grab it, but Gordon yanked it away and glared at Briggs.

Gordon then reached out and plucked an ear plug out of Briggs' ear, adjusted the instrument and played a discordant chord that sounded like the end of time. The ripping reverberation of ear-shattering feedback made Briggs' hair stand on end. He winced in pain and covered his ears.

People in the audience started to cry out in agony.

"Please get back, boogaloo," said Gordon.

Briggs had a confused expression on his face. He looked out at the audience as he backed away. The once peaceful crowd of smiling faces had changed. The faces were now full of rage and anger. Eyes glaring, they charged the stage. "Kill! Kill!"

Briggs and the FBI men were in shock as the crowd came at them like an angry mob.

"Oops. Too much feedback," said Gordon as he adjusted his instrument again.

"What did you just do?" asked Devon.

"I must have hit the wrong chord there," said Gordon as he took Devon by the arm and led him off the stage, along with Huddleson and Janice. "I just wanted to distract them a bit. The FBI guy. I kinda over-did it."

"Yeah, ya think? We have to get out of here," said Devon.

Briggs, with his ears still ringing, whirled around in a rage but Gordon was gone. Briggs looked back across the stage and saw the crowd climbing onto the platform. The faces of those in front looked like sick junkies craving a fix.

Huddleson had his coat draped over Gordon as he, Devon and Janice snuck through the frenzied crowd which was starting to tear the stage apart. FBI agents combed through the crowd looking for Gordon. One agent thought he saw him and tapped a large figure on the shoulder. The figure turned around and the agent found himself staring at a huge punk rocker who actually looked much more menacing than Gordon.

As Devon led the concealed Gordon through the crowd Gordon tried to get him to stop. "I was just getting warmed up ya know," said Gordon.

"We can't stay here," pleaded Devon.

"Probably shoulda tried a smaller hall first," said

Gordon. "A nice lounge, perhaps."

"Can we have this conversation later?" said Devon, dragging Gordon along. All around the stadium, FBI Agents, wearing headsets, were sealing off exits to the stadium. Devon, Gordon, Huddleson and Janice were getting close to one of the exits when they saw a problem. Every exit had armed guards standing next to them.

"They've got the exits sealed," cried Janice. "We'll never get out of here."

"Follow me," said Gordon as he started to climb the steps leading to the top of the stadium.

"Where do you think you're going?" asked Devon.

"You want outta here, right?"

Gordon proceeded up the stairs with Devon, Janice and Huddleson behind him. Out of breath and sweating, they reached the nosebleed seats that looked out over the huge stadium. In the other direction lay a giant parking lot and various roads leading out of it. Several highways leading toward New York were still backed up with traffic. Devon looked down at the lot 150 feet below.

"I don't think this was such a good idea," said Devon.

"You wanted a way out," said Gordon.

"Out of the stadium, not out of life as we know it," answered Devon.

"I sense a basic problem," said Huddleson. He turned toward Gordon, "You can fly, right?"

"Can't everybody?" He then broke down laughing. "Got ya, didn't I? Fly. I wish."

"So, what's the plan?" asked Devon.

"Hold on to my back," said Gordon, straddling the top of the stadium wall.

"Ah. Are you sure about this?" asked Devon.

"What about us?" asked Janice.

"Yeah," added Huddleson.

"Nobody's shooting at you. You can just walk outta here."

"But we climbed all those stairs," said Huddleson.

"I can't carry all of you," said Gordon.

"Gordon's right," said Devon. "We'll have to meet up somewhere once we're in the clear. Sorry guys. You made the climb for nothing."

"Nothing? I wouldn't miss this for the world," said Janice.

"Miss what?" asked Devon.

"Whatever it is he's gonna do."

It then hit Devon that what he was about to do was insane.

"What exactly *are* we going to do?" asked Devon.

"You doubt my abilities?" smiled Gordon.

"Ah..."

"Doubt is gravity for the soul, my boy," said Gordon.

"Well, it's gravity right now that I'm afraid of."

Gordon looked thoughtful.

"Upon further reflection...there's no need to carry you, after all. We'll do this instead."

Gordon smiled, aimed his instrument at the parking lot in a 45 degree angle and hit a metallic chord. The vibration shot through the night air like a harpoon, causing something strange to happen to the dust particles in its way. A thin line formed almost out of nothing and then the line turned into a glimmering wire.

"Follow me," said Gordon as he hooked himself onto the wire and slid to the lot below.

Devon took off his belt and swung it over the wire. "Get on my back," he said to Janice, who wrapped her arms around his neck and her legs around his waist.

Holding on to both ends of the belt, Devon followed Gordon down the glimmering wire to the parking lot with Huddleson right behind him. As soon as they landed, the line crackled and faded away.

Devon looked back at the disappearing wire. "How'd you do that?"

"A-minor," said Gordon. "You can also use a B-flat, but it's not as strong."

"No. I mean, how does hitting a chord on that guitar or whatever it is do that?"

"You mean, like, how-on-a-physics-quiz, how?

"Yeah."

"Well, first, I set this for high." He adjusted a knob on his instrument. "Then I dial this up to intensity laser sonic, and hit a chord—in this case A-minor—and *zap*. The sound wave magnifies to the point that it solidifies the molecules in its path.

"If you wanta know how that happens, it's in a book somewhere. I forget where I left it."

"Look!" screamed Janice. They looked back at the gates to the arena and saw soldiers pouring through and spreading out into the parking lot.

"We can't stay here," said Devon.

"What are we gonna do with him?" Janice nodded to Gordon.

"We need a place where he won't be noticed," offered Devon.

I know just the spot," said Professor Huddleson.

CHAPTER EIGHTEEN

On any given night on Manhattan's Lower East-side at the corner of Second Avenue and St. Mark's Square, you will find what is affectionately known as the "freak parade." Some of the strangest looking people on the planet live, work and party down in an ever-changing neighborhood of aging hippies, nex-gen millionaires and working class elite who gather nightly to see and be seen among the punk rock Mecca of the universe.

Gordon, Devon, Janice and Professor Huddleson stepped out of a subway exit on the corner and looked around at the human circus unfolding around them. Girls in green and purple hair and men and women tattooed from eyebrows to toenails, blended with a scattering of tourists in business casual. Basically, Gordon fit right in while Devon, Janice and Huddleson looked out of place.

"Not in Kansas anymore, are we Toto?" quipped Devon.

Gordon was standing in front of an apartment building when a young woman in spiked, bleach-blonde hair and a leather necklace stepped out of the building.

Gordon immediately noticed that the woman

was one, very attractive and two, was pushing against the inside of her cheek with her tongue. She also had a grimace of pain on her face as she looked up from her purse and found Gordon standing in front of her, blocking her way.

"I'm in love," smiled Gordon.

"Out of my way, asshole," snapped the woman.

Huddleson gave Devon a look and nodded toward Gordon. "I think we should keep a low profile."

"Ahhh, Gordon," said Devon.

Gordon stepped aside but as the woman pushed by him, he reached out and grabbed her wrist.

"I can fix that, you know," said Gordon.

"Get your hand off me." Gordon let go. "Now beat it, dick head."

The woman started to walk away and Gordon was about to follow her when Devon stepped in front of him.

"Excuse me, Gordon," said Devon. "What are you doing?"

Gordon ignored Devon's question and stepped around him and caught up with the woman.

"That must really hurt," he said, now walking beside her. The woman stopped, whirled around and put her hands on her hips.

"Are you deaf, donkey breath?"

"Is it throbbing?" asked Gordon.

Devon decided he'd better intervene quickly so he approached Gordon and the woman with a look of embarrassment on his face.

"I have to apologize for my friend. He's not from around here," said Devon.

The woman's eyes widened in anger and she looked like she was ready to kill someone. Devon stepped back as she opened her mouth, but nothing came out. Instead of talking, she held her jaw and cried out, "Aggghh!"

Gordon adjusted his instrument and strummed the strings. He directed the vibrations at the woman's mouth, which, for a brief second glowed red then blue. The woman's expression of agony washed away. She stared at Gordon in awestruck wonder. She held her mouth and opened and closed it, running her tongue over her teeth. Her look quickly turned to one of confusion and then suspicion.

"What did you do?"

Janice stepped up, smiling. "He's an alien. A nice alien. He heals people."

The woman touched her jaw, looked at Gordon who just smiled and shrugged.

The woman looked from Gordon to Devon and finally to Janice. "What did you say?"

"I said…" started Janice, but Devon stopped her.

"He's just visiting," said Devon. "He didn't mean anything…I mean…what exactly did he do? I'm not sure."

"He made the pain go away, I think," said the woman. "With that," she added pointing at Gordon's instrument. "How did you do that?"

"It was nothing," said Gordon. "A little G-major. But you should still get that tooth looked at. It's probably abscessed if it hurt that much. I might be able to actually heal it if you let me strum a few more chords."

"Yeah, right," said the woman. "That sound, though. I've heard it somewhere before."

"More like everywhere," said Janice. "Where have you been, lady? This is the dude. This is where the music comes from."

"Ever since my tooth started to hurt I haven't been out much. You're not making a lot sense."

"Don't you listen to the radio?"

"Not if I can help it."

"So you've never heard his music?" asked Devon.

"How is that even possible?" said Huddleson.

"What can I tell you, my tooth really hurt, or it did until he did his, you know, G-major thing. I'm feeling a little dizzy. Must be my low blood sugar. Since I developed this tooth problem, I haven't been able to eat for days. I was just headed to this great chili place just around the corner."

"Lead the way," said Gordon. "I could go for a bite."

"Ah, is that such a good idea?" asked Huddleson.

"Even aliens have to eat you know," whispered Gordon. "Come on. Besides, I love chili."

The sign on the outside of the tiny restaurant read "Exterminator Chili."

"My name's Sharon, by the way," said the woman with spiked hair as she led them to a booth in the rear. Gordon, Devon, Janice and Huddleson each introduced themselves as they slid into the booth. The restaurant was decorated in early 50s mode of tackiness with an over-abundance of Elvis memorabilia.

"How'd you know my tooth was abscessed?" asked Sharon.

"Are you kidding? I could almost feel it myself," said Gordon.

"You some kinda new wave dentist?"

"I'm a rock star."

Devon put his hands over his face.

"Yeah, and I'm Madonna."

Sharon looked at Devon, Janice and Huddleson and then back at Gordon. "What's wrong with this picture?" she asked.

"What do you mean?" said Janice.

"I mean I get him," she said, nodding at Gordon, "but what are *you* three doing here?"

"How'd you like to have my baby?" asked Gordon.

Sharon spilled a bottle of salsa. Huddleson cleared his throat.

"I don't know about you guys but I'm starving," said Janice.

"I could go for an amino acid-complex carbo combo with a dash of d. How about you?" Gordon smiled at Sharon.

Sharon stared at Gordon and then at Devon and the others. "Ya know. I just realized. I'm supposed to be someplace."

She started to get up when Gordon plucked a string and Sharon felt herself yanked back down by unseen forces. Her eyes widened as she looked around to see what happened.

"Okay. Maybe I'll stay a few minutes."

A waitress in her mid-50s strolled over and slapped five menus down on the table.

"Our specials are on the board over da counter. Da rest is on da menu. Ya want anyting ta drink?"

"I'd like a bottle of the strongest stuff you got," said Sharon.

"All we got is beer."

"A dozen beers and a straw, then," said Sharon.

The waitress left and Gordon slid closer to Sharon and looked her over. "You sure are pretty. It's been a long time for me."

"You just get outta prison?"

"Been doin some traveling," said Gordon. "If you had one wish, what would it be?"

"I stopped wishing a long time ago," said Sharon.

"There must be something you want," said Gordon.

"There's plenty. I just stopped wishing for it."

"What do you want more than anything else?"

Sharon smiled. "To be young again."

"How young would you like to be?"

"Twenty-five would be nice."

"Where I come from, we have a custom," said Gordon. "If one person grants another person a wish, the other person has to grant a wish back."

"Figures. Is this guy for real?"

"I told you," said Janice. "He's an alien."

"She means a foreigner," said Devon. "He's actually from New Zealand."

"With lots of zeal I gather," said Sharon. "So, you're gonna make me twenty-five again."

"That depends. You haven't heard my wish yet."

"I don't have to hear it. I can almost feel it," smiled Sharon seductively and slightly mocking Gordon's previous remark about her painful tooth.

"Maybe we should go back to your apartment."

"I haven't had my chili yet," said Sharon.

Gordon grinned at her.

"Why don't you get it to go?"

CHAPTER NINETEEN

Brigss *paced back and* forth in front in the interrogation room at the FBI field office. Edgar French was sitting at a table with Powell standing in a corner, observing.

"Where are they?" asked Briggs finally.

"How the hell should I know?" said Edgar. "I told you. I just met the kid and he played me his music. This Gordon dude. Never heard of him. You say he's the one responsible for that sound? Man he's good. But I still don't understand why I'm here."

Briggs glared at Edgar then turned toward Agent Powell and nodded.

"Mr. French," said Agent Powell. "I don't think you understand the trouble you're in. You're already facing a conspiracy charge. How would you like aiding and abetting?"

"Hey. What's one more trumped-up charge between friends?" said Edgar.

"What was it you said you were again?" asked Briggs.

"A musicologist, and part-time programming consultant. My musicology gig doesn't quite cover my expenses if you know what I mean," said Edgar.

Briggs turned to Agent Powell. "Get this idiot out

of here. Go back to the city. If I was going to hide, that's where I'd go."

M*eanwhile, in a* basement office in the Pentagon, Colonel Pemberton read over some reports quickly and put them down just as the phone rang. He picked up the receiver and spoke.

"Pemberton."

"Where's our asset?" said a voice on the phone.

"The FBI spooked him," said Pemberton. "But he can't go far. We'll find him."

"I expect you to take care of it."

"I will."

CHAPTER TWENTY

At *Exterminator Chili*, Devon stared at the two empty spaces in the booth while Huddleson ate his chili.

"Maybe I should have gone with him," suggested Devon.

"I think right now, he'd like to be alone," said Huddleson, looking closely at his spoon of industrial strength chicken chili.

"Am I the only one who feels uncomfortable about this?" asked Devon.

"I tried to tell her," said Janice. "But you had to knock it down."

"You want her to know that the man she's taking home is an extraterrestrial?"

"What if he's—you know, built funny?" asked Janice.

Devon made an ugly face. "Oooo. You've got a point."

"What do you think this is?" asked Huddleson, holding a long black curved object between his thumb and forefinger. "It was in my chili."

The waitress just happened to be walking by and leaned down. "That's a toasted Peruvian chili pepper. Gives it a kick, don't it?"

Around the corner and on the second floor of a pre-war building, the sounds of soft music and squeaky bed-springs flowed through the half-opened window of a room whose light appeared to brighten and dim then glow a bright red to the sharp squeals and gasps of a female.

"Oh, oh oh my God," shouted Sharon. "It's...oh...oh...OH!"

The light in the room glowed bright then faded. Lying in a bed that took up the entire room, Sharon stared up at the ceiling then turned toward Gordon who was lying next to her.

Sharon looked about ten years younger. Both she and Gordon had calm relaxed smiles on their faces.

"You're gonna think I'm crazy," said Sharon. "But, hah, for a second there, I almost thought your...ah...you know...was glowing."

"I don't know about me glowing," smiled Gordon, "but you sure are."

Sharon kissed Gordon's forehead. Suddenly it hit her. She looked down at herself. Her eyes widened as she leapt off the bed and went into the bathroom.

The reflection in the mirror was of a woman ten years younger.

"Sonofabitch." She pinched the skin on her face to make sure it was real. She tried to make crows feet but couldn't.

"They're gone," she squealed.

Sharon returned to the bedroom to find Gordon getting dressed. "Hey. You wanta go for twenty?" she asked.

Gordon smiled, reached down next to the bed

and brought up his instrument. He strummed a chord, filling the room with harmonic sounds, then stopped.

"You're fine the way you are. Come on, get dressed."

"Where are we going?' asked Sharon.

"Up on the roof. It's time to put on another concert," said Gordon. "My first one was a bust."

Down on the street, Devon, Janice and Huddleson stood outside the door to Sharon's building. Devon hit the buzzer. No answer.

"Now where'd they go?' As if in an answer, the sound filled the air above their heads. Devon and the others looked around and then up at the roof of the building.

"He's on the roof," shouted Devon as he buzzed every apartment until someone buzzed them in.

By the time Devon and the others reached the roof, Gordon was already playing to a group of bikers, rappers and heavy metal rockers. Janice was the first to notice Sharon's youthfulness. Janice smiled at Sharon and Sharon smiled back. Everyone was turned toward Gordon as he played a beautiful ballad.

The music began to attract a larger crowd as more and more people poured through the doorway onto the roof until every inch of space was taken. When the roof was filled other nearby roofs filled with people, mesmerized by the healing sounds emanating from Gordon's instrument. Even a group Hells Angels poured out of a nearby rooftop door, looking ready for battle, but then Gordon strummed his instrument and each of the Hells Angels smiled and settled down.

Powell and Agent Duggin were walking down a street when something caught Powell's attention.

"Did you hear that?" he asked.

"Hear what?" asked Duggin.

Powell looked up toward the rooftops of the city and nodded. "It's the sound. We're close."

Gordon finished playing his song and the audience was entranced. Just then one of the rappers whispered something in Gordon's ear and Gordon nodded a "yes."

He waved Devon over. "Devon, my man. I just got a request to play something a little different."

"I think we'd all appreciate a little change," said Devon.

"Okay, then. Take a seat." Devon sat down next to Gordon as he started to play a familiar rap beat and shuffle on the instrument. "Whatta ya think?"

"Go for it."

"I'm gonna need a little help here," said Gordon. "You dudes back there."

The rappers looked at each other.

"Yeah you. Start shufflin out a beat."

The rappers scraped their feet on the roof top, sounding just like scratches in a rap song. Gordon picked up a rhythm on his instrument.

"In the beginning," sang Gordon,
"Before anyone was around,
Before anything else,
There was a sound.
And that sound lit a spark,
And it was no longer dark.
And when there was light,
That light shined so bright.
You could see from afar,
That light was a star.
And from that star,
There came a sound.
And that sound.
It cut like a knife.
From that sound
came life.
As we evolved
And wove sound into song,
The music pulled us together,
And we all sang along.
This music, like all sound,
Has vibrations that heal,
But if you hit the wrong chord,
It can kill like a sword.
So be careful my friend.
Play only tunes that mend.
To help those near and afar.
With this Sound from a Star."

"Oh, baby" shouted a rapper. "You got that right."

The audience applauded and Gordon immediately went into some funky rock and roll.

✦

D*own on the street*, Powell had gathered several agents around him. They followed the music until a look of concern crossed his face. "Wait," said Powell, putting a hand to his ear. "We're close."

He glanced around and then up toward the roof of the apartment building he was standing in front of. Above the roof, the sky was lit up like the Northern Lights.

"We found him," smiled Powell.

"Should I call Briggs?' asked Duggin.

"We can take him," said Powell.

O*n the roof*, Gordon played another soulful tune, mesmerizing the audience. Devon turned to Huddleson and snapped his fingers, bringing him out of a trance.

"Hey. Snap out of it."

Huddleson blinked at Devon.

"He doesn't even know how powerful he is," said Devon. "How much good he could do."

"I wouldn't be so sure of that," said Huddleson.

"Where ever he's from, it's obvious they're more advanced than we are," said Devon. "I'm just worried about what we're gonna do with him. We can't stay up here forever."

"Why not?" smiled Huddleson, still stoned on the music.

"And with the FBI trying to kill him..."

"We don't want to *kill* him," said Powell.

Devon whirled around as Powell and several other FBI agents with their guns drawn stepped out of the shadows at the edge of the roof.

"We just wanta talk to him," said Powell.

Powell nodded and the other agents aimed their weapons at Gordon ready to fire when Devon ran to Gordon's side.

"So, if you'd be so kind as to put down your...whatever it is, and come with us," urged Powell.

Gordon looked at Devon. "A fella could get the idea he's not very welcome around here. What is it? Do I smell funny? Break a union rule? I don't get it."

"Please step away from the boy," warned the FBI agent.

"All I wanted was to play a few gigs," said Gordon. "Make some music. But noooooo. What is it with you guys?"

"Come over here, son," beckoned Powell.

Devon looked at Powell and then at Gordon. Devon lowered his head and then started to walk toward the FBI when Gordon grabbed him by the wrist and pulled him toward him, holding the instrument behind Devon.

"Okay. Nobody move or I hit E-minor."

Powell looked at Duggin and the other agents and then at Gordon.

"E-minor?"

Gordon struck a sour chord that sent a ripple of electricity across the roof to the water tower on the next building, causing the tower to explode.

The agents ducked down and covered their heads as wood and water fell from the sky. Powell looked over at Gordon.

"E-minor. Wanta try for a B-flat?"

Powell just stared at the empty space where the water tower used to be.

"You can put your guns down now," ordered Gordon, waving the instrument in their direction. Powell put his weapon down and indicated that the other agents do so as well.

"Okay, Devon and I are gonna go now. Nothing's gonna happen to the boy if you all play ball."

Gordon moved Devon to the side of the roof. Devon exchanged a glance with Janice and Huddleson. Janice looked worried. Sharon was holding on to her. Devon and Gordon reached the edge of the roof. It appeared to be as far as they could go. Devon looked at Gordon and then down fifteen stories and then across to several other rooftops. He looked at Gordon who seemed to be measuring a distance with his hands.

"Don't worry, Pal. I won't let anything happen to you. I just don't know what else to do right now."

"I think another A-minor might be in order," suggested Devon.

Gordon smiled at Devon and raised his eyebrows. Gordon hit his magic chord. Only this time it was a fuller strum than at the stadium. Instead of a line, a platform appeared, stretching from the top of the roof to the next roof of the next building. The agents and everyone else on the roof gasped. Devon and Gordon started to leave when Janice tried to run toward them, but an FBI agent grabbed her.

"Devon!"

Devon waved to Janice and then followed Gordon across the platform which seemed to be made from solidified air. Devon looked down and saw nothing but air beneath his feet, but it had a shimmering quality as he walked across it.

"Tell Mom not to worry!" Devon called to Janice.

Powell and some agents started to follow but as soon as they got to the edge, the platform shivered and then disappeared.

An agent held Powell back from falling fifteen stories as the platform vanished. The FBI agents looked on in wonder as Devon and Gordon ran off. Gordon hit A-minors as they jumped from rooftop to rooftop until they faded into the night.

"You see that?" Powell turned to Duggin.

Janice started crying as Sharon put an arm around her.

"Hey. Take it easy."

Sharon wiped a tear from her eye as Huddleson took in a deep breath.

"He'll be all right," said Huddleson.

"All right? My best friend's just been kidnapped by an alien!" shouted Janice.

They were about twenty blocks south of the roof where Gordon had been playing, when Devon and

Gordon finally stopped and looked back. Devon caught his breath and was about to sit down when Gordon pointed to the horizon.

"Uh, oh." A squadron of helicopters appeared in the western sky.

"*I fought the law and the law won...*" sang Gordon, who had a pensive look on his face. "Okay, it's time for you to boogie on down the road."

"What?"

"Scram. Beat it. Go on. Get outta here."

Devon looked at Gordon and then at the choppers. "What are ya gonna do?"

"I figure I can take out one, maybe two before they get me," Gordon tuned his instrument. "You better get going."

"Where am I supposed to go?"

"Go home."

"I've got nothing to go home to."

"Hey, I don't care where you go," said Gordon. "But show time is over. Now beat it."

"I'm not leaving you here."

"I'm not staying here."

"I'm going with you then."

"I travel alone, kid."

"Look. It's my fault you're even here."

Gordon turned the instrument toward Devon.

"You're gettin to be a bit of pain now, Devon."

"Oh, yeah. Well so are you. You think you're gonna go down like King Kong or something. Just like that? Well then I'm goin', too. I can be just as suicidal as you. Because I'll level with ya, you're the only thing I can think of that's worth livin for right now and if you go, then I don't wanta be here."

Gordon looked at Devon, his anger dissolving into compassion.

"I'm not gonna surrender."

"Who said anything about giving up?"

"You got a better idea?"

"Hit us an A-minor and get us off this roof."

Just then the choppers swooped down over the roof top, spotlights criss-crossing across the night-time sky. Devon climbed on Gordon's back.

"Oh sheeeiit!" Gordon screamed as he hit another A-minor chord. A line of vibrating air formed down the side of a building just as the choppers opened fire. Gordon and Devon slid down the line as bullets passed just behind them.

When they reached the ground, Gordon let Devon off his back. "Okay champ, now what?"

CHAPTER TWENTY-ONE

Spider, the spaced-out DJ, was fast asleep in the fetal position, curled up on a large turntable, spinning around and around slowly when Devon and Gordon arrived. Gordon strummed a simple B-flat that knocked Spider off the turntable and onto his feet, eyes wide open.

"Jesus Joseph and Mary! What was that sound, man?" asked a dazed Spider.

Devon stepped in front of him as Spider furrowed his brow.

"You."

"I got somebody here you might wanta meet," said Devon, standing aside and revealing Gordon and his instrument. Gordon played another chord, lighting up the studio in bright heavenly light. Spider dropped down on his knees and kissed Gordon's hand.

Gordon looked embarrassed as he pulled his hand away.

"Oh man. It's you." Spider bent lower and began to kiss Gordon's feet.

"Okay, Spider, that's enough," said Gordon, stepping away.

"We need your help," said Devon. .

Spider stood up and grinned from ear to ear. "You got it man, anything."

Back on the East Village rooftop, Powell was conversing with Duggin while Huddleson tried to calm down an anxious Janice, with a little help from Sharon, when a helicopter descended from above and landed on the roof. Briggs stepped out and looked around at the motley group still assembled. He shook his head and walked over to Powell.

"You just let him get away?" asked Briggs.

"He took a hostage," said Powell.

A gust of wind got Briggs attention and he and Powell turned to look up and saw a squadron of Army helicopters circling the building.

"Where did they come from?"

"Beats me, Chief," said Powell.

As if on cue, one of the choppers broke away from the others and landed on the roof next to the FBI helicopter. Out of a side doorway where a machine gunner cradled an M-50, Colonel Pemberton appeared and jumped down to the roof. Holding his hat in one hand and ducking under the blades, the Colonel marched over to Powell and Briggs.

"We'll take it from here," said the Colonel.

"The hell you will," said Briggs.

"You don't know what you're dealing with," said Colonel Pemberton.

"And you do?"

✦

A *bus painted black with* a lightning bolt stenciled on the roof pulled into an ally behind the radio station where Spider worked and stopped at a white door. On the side of the bus, which was the kind of bus rock-groups used to tour with the windows painted over, was some lettering that read "Thundering Herd." As soon as the doors of the bus opened, the white door opened and Devon and Gordon stepped out and climbed on the bus. The doors of the bus closed behind them and the bus pulled away.

Devon and Gordon found themselves facing a bus load of heavy metal rockers, still wearing their face makeup. The leader of the group was dressed like a Gene Simmons/Kiss wannabe. He was tall and sweaty, giving off a sour odor that smelled like a blend of cheap cosmetics and under-arm perspiration. The leader approached Devon and Gordon and turned toward Gordon.

"Spider says you play a mean guitar," said the leader.

"He's too kind," responded Gordon.

"Who's the boy?"

"My assistant."

The band leader looked Devon up and down and licked his blackened lips, then smiled. He reached out and grabbed Devon's arm and pulled. "He's my assistant now."

"Get your hands off me," shouted Devon.

The band leader held Devon tighter. Gordon reached out and put his hand on Devon's shoulder.

"Let him go," said Gordon.

"Let's get one thing straight. I'm the leader of this tribe. You want to ride on my bus, play my songs, then you do what I say. Otherwise, you can get off right now," spat the leader.

Gordon looked at Devon and removed his hand from his shoulder. Devon looked at Gordon helplessly. "Kid was starting to get on my nerves anyway," said Gordon.

Devon's eyes widened.

"That's more like it," said the band leader. "Here." And he shoved Devon back at Gordon. "You can have him till I need him. I don't know if Spider told you, but we gotta hit thirty-four cities in thirty-five days. So, if I was you, I'd catch some zzz's while we're rollin, 'cause when we stop, everybody bops." With that, the band leader walked to the rear of the bus laughing to himself.

Devon turned to Gordon. "You were just going to let him have me?"

"Take it easy," said Gordon. "We're here, aren't we? This was your idea, remember? Besides, if he tried anything funny, I would have E-minored his balls."

Devon smiled as he settled down in a seat and Gordon took the seat next to him. As the bus started to pull out of the alley, Devon turned to Gordon. "You're not what I expected."

"Just what did you expect—a little green fella with big eyes and a finger that glows red?"

"I don't know."

Gordon made a face at Devon with his eyes bulging. Gordon smiled to himself and took out his instrument. As the bus moved through the city's deserted streets, he began to stroke the strings, looking out the window.

"We're gonna play us some rock and roll," said Gordon.

As the bus drove off into the night Devon looked out at the darkness, and the expression on his face reflected the fear and confusion he felt inside. He turned back to Gordon.

"Where did you come from?"

"Originally?"

"Originally."

"My mother."

Devon stared at Gordon.

"Sorry," smiled Gordon. "Actually, it's a lot like this place, but not as much fun."

"How did you get here? Do you have a space ship?"

"A what?"

"A vehicle. Transportation. I mean how did you get to our planet?"

"Oh that's easy. Teleportation."

"How does that work, exactly?"

"Beats the hell out of me. Ask an astrophysicist. I'm a sound man, myself. You wantta know about sound, I got ya covered. Teleportation. Nada. Just know it beats hitch-hiking."

"Huh?"

"Ah, that was a joke."

"So you just got beamed here, right?"

"Beamed? Not a term I recognize."

"Whenever I've heard the term teleportation

used it meant that something, or in your case, someone, was virtually transmitted like a beam of light or electricity, from one spot to another."

"Well that just sounds impossible," said Gordon.

"So then how do you do it?"

"I just go to the teleport and buy a ticket."

"You're not gonna tell me are ya?"

"I just did."

"What are you back on your planet, some kind of doctor?"

"Doctor? Good heavens, no. I'm a street singer. Got run outta the last place I was in."

"So, basically you're a vagrant, a bum."

"Hey. I work. Gotta admit though, I never got the response there that I got here. Even though it was a little mixed, wasn't it? I mean some folks really liked me and then those other guys. They wanted to shoot me."

Devon shook his head and looked back out the window as the city passed behind them and they drove over a bridge heading west.

CHAPTER TWENTY-TWO

*I*t *didn't take long for* the bus tour to become of blur of stadiums, set ups, sound checks, performances and then breakdowns, re-loading the bus and on to the next venue. Devon would watch from the side of the stage as the band played hard and heavy metal rock numbers. Gordon managed to blend right in, pounding out heavy rifts with a vengeance. The band leader seemed to be enjoying Gordon's participation. He even gave him a guitar solo every now and then.

As Devon helped other roadies assemble and disassemble the equipment it began to sink in that the music this band played was the antithesis of the music Gordon played before. There were no harmonic melodies, only heavy metal rifts that chopped through the night like musical weapons, cutting down everything in their path. No one was getting healed in the audience. In fact, there were mostly fights and body slamming.

It all seemed to be taking its toll on Gordon and during a break in the fourth sold-out show, Devon approached Gordon.

"You don't look so good," said Devon.

"Whatta ya mean?"

"I think it's the music. It's making you sick."

"It's a little raw, I'll admit, but the audience seems to like it."

"This audience is so strung out on speed and God-knows-what that they'd like a buzz saw cutting through a car engine."

"Rock and roll."

"But what about the healing?"

"What about it?"

"Donchu miss it?" said Devon. "I wanta show you something."

Devon started walking off the stage.

"Hey, where are you going?" shouted Gordon.

Devon kept walking until he reached the top of a row of seats on back of the stage. Gordon caught up with him and they both looked back down at the stadium and the thousands of screaming fans.

"I gotta get back down there. The band just returned."

"Just look out there first."

Devon pointed to a nearby hill. Gordon looked outside the stadium and the land surrounding it where he saw a bleak picture of dying trees and burned out buildings.

"I think it's the chords you have to play for heavy metal music. They must have some kind of anti-life force or something. You're killing these people and they don't know it, or even care. Look over there."

Devon pointed at a tree that was dying, its leaves drooping and falling to the ground.

"An hour ago, that tree was fine."

"Now you're telling *me* about *my* music. Hey

Devon. Maybe it's time for you to go home to your mother," snapped Gordon, and he left and returned to the stage to join the others.

As Devon watched him leave, he knew that something was happening to Gordon. He was becoming harder edged, with darker circles under his eyes. There was a viciousness to his expressions.

Devon watched as Gordon walked among the fans, the heavy metal, leather rockers, who slam danced and butted heads as he passed by toward the stage.

At another concert, the audience stormed the stage and members of the band smashed their instruments over the heads of crazed fans to protect themselves. The entire concert turned into a brawl. Devon looked up to see Gordon about to crash his instrument down on the head of a young man...when they locked eyes. Devon turned away. Gordon was about to swing...when he stopped. He looked over to where Devon had been standing, only Devon was gone.

The fan started taunting Gordon, urging him to hit him. Gordon again got ready to swing, but then stopped. Something shifted in his eyes and Gordon lowered his instrument. He looked around at the destruction on the stage, then looked in the distance where Devon was walking under a light about to leave the stadium. A realization registered on Gordon's face. He looked around at the melee and then set off in the direction Devon was heading.

Devon was walking alone down the highway when he heard a sound. He turned around just as the tour bus pulled up alongside him and the door opened. Devon ignored it until...

"Take a ride on my magic bus," shouted Gordon. Devon turned toward the bus and saw Gordon behind the wheel.

"I'm a lover, not a fighter, babe," smiled Gordon. "Come on. Get in."

Devon let out a sigh, then smiled and climbed on board.

"You stole the bus?" asked Devon.

"I figure, why even bother to ask for it, right? Besides, the leader was an A-one asshole. He doesn't deserve this bus."

Gordon stepped on the gas and they started off down the highway. Devon sat down and looked outside at the night and the open road. Gordon looked back at him and smiled.

CHAPTER TWENTY-THREE

At the *New Jersey FBI* bureau headquarters, Briggs stared out his window at what was turning into a miserable day weather-wise as well as any other way you wanted to measure it. His "most wanted" had fled to parts unknown and he still didn't have a clue about what he was chasing. Was it man or an alien? Just then the door to his office opened and Agent Powell stepped in.

"We found him," said Powell.

"Where is he?'

"He stole a bus. According to the bus's Lojak locator, he's in Clearwater, North Carolina."

"Then why are you standing here?"

The bus turned off a four-lane highway just outside Clearwater. Devon stared out the window at the farms and rows of orange trees. Then, a sign caught his eye as the bus rolled along. It read: "Revival. Come and Be Healed. Follow signs. Five miles."

"That's it," said Devon. "Gordon, turn the bus around."

"What is it? What did you see?"

"Just turn around take the next right down that

two-lane road."

As Gordon did a U-turn in the middle of the highway, he turned toward Devon. "You oughta call your folks. Tell 'em you're all right."

"I'd rather let them worry," said Devon. "See that sign? Turn down that road there."

Gordon looked at the revival sign and shook his head. "You're kidding, right?"

"It's what you need to do."

Gordon hit the brakes and pulled the bus off to the side of the road.

"I'll make you a deal. You tell me what you're running away from, and I'll go to the revival."

"My parents are getting a divorce," said Devon, looking slightly ashamed.

"That explains a lot."

"A lot of what?" asked Devon.

"A lot of what makes you tick," said Gordon, removing the brake and giving the bus some gas. As it surged forward, he continued. "I thought maybe you were some kind of psychopath with a death wish. Turns out you're just another normal angst-filled teenager."

"What are you now," demanded Devon. "Shrink from a star?"

"You should go home, Devon. Your parents need you."

"Need me? Most of the time, they don't even know I'm alive. I don't know why they ever got married."

"Where I come from there's only one reason to get married."

"What's that?"

"The connection. To be whole. To be healed."

"Take me there, then. I don't wanta go home."

Gordon turned off the road at the sign and began heading toward the revival.

"We'll see."

Back in the East Village in Manhattan, Sharon was painting something on the wall over her bedroom. She had a paint brush in one hand and a bottle of Jim Beam in the other. She finished her painting and then went to the window and looked up at the stars. Just then her door buzzer buzzed. She let out a sigh and walked to the door.

"Who's there?"

"It's us," said Professor Huddleson and Janice.

Sharon opened the door quickly and stood back as they burst in, both wearing wide smiles.

"They're back?" said Sharon hopefully.

"Not exactly," said Huddleson. "I just got a call. We have a taxi waiting to take us to the airport."

"Where are we going?"

"South."

Janice looked at the wall where Sharon was painting and saw the 'words: "'Take a chance on getting slapped, you might get kissed.'

"What does that mean," asked Janice.

"You'll know soon enough," smiled Sharon. "I'm ready. Let's go."

✦

Flares lit up the North Carolina highway surrounding the tour bus, along with several police cars. The band leader strutted around, looking like an angry rooster.

"They're gonna pay for this."

The band leader kicked a tire and then turned as a government sedan pulled up. The back door opened and Briggs climbed out. Powell got out of the driver's side as other FBI agents pulled up next to them in black SUVs. The band leader turned toward them.

"I expect a full reimbursement on anything missing from my bus. Who are you guys?"

"Briggs. FBI. That it?"

"What do the Feds care about somebody stealing a bus?" asked the band leader.

A highway patrolman approached the FBI agents.

"We were monitoring the scanner and found it an hour ago."

"They gotta be close by, then," said Briggs. "How far's Charlotte from here?"

"We got an all-points," said the patrolman.

"Pictures everywhere," said Briggs. "I want every lawman in the state on this one."

"What'd he do?" asked the patrolman.

"He stole my bus," said the band leader.

"I don't give a shit about your bus, asshole," shouted Briggs. "Who is this guy?'

"So what did the fugitives do?" asked the patrolman again.

"Do? They pissed me off," said Briggs, who was

about to storm off when a military Humvee pulled up and Colonel Pemberton got out.

"Oh, geez," said Briggs. "Not this birdbrain."

Pemberton walked over to Briggs and said, "Briggs. Could I have a word? Alone?"

Briggs nodded to Powell who motioned to the band leader to follow him.

"Let me take your statement," said Powell to the band leader.

As soon as Pemberton and Briggs were alone, the Colonel whispered something to Briggs, and his eyes widened. Briggs put his hand to his head as a sick looked washed over his face.

"You knew this all along," snapped Briggs.

The Colonel looked away and then back at Briggs. "I'm sorry. I was hoping we could contain it, but things have gotten out of hand. I felt you should know what we're up against."

A *few hours later*, a rental car sped down the same highway where the bus had been found. It skidded to a stop next to the "Revival" sign. Inside the car were Professor Huddleson, Janice and Sharon. Huddleson was driving. He lowered his window and stared up at the sign.

"That must be it."

"A revival?"

"A born-again extraterrestrial?"

"That's where Devon told us to meet him."

Huddleson made the turn and started down the narrow roadway, past fields of corn and cotton, woods and swamps. Five miles later, they came into a clearing and saw a huge tent.

A large crowd had gathered at the revival meeting. Cars were parked haphazardly in all directions out from the revival tent. At the entrance to the tent, Devon and Gordon were talking to a man in his mid-50s, who called himself Reverend Petri, like the dish.

"Brother Devon," said the Reverend. "You have to understand, I'm not denying this man has the gift. I'm just saying this is my congregation. They have come to believe in me."

"We don't wanta take your congregation, Reverend. We just wanta help you."

"If I let a stranger, someone they do not know, attempt to do God's healing and God forbid for some reason, something goes wrong..."

Gordon looked at all the people pouring into the tent.

"He can heal the lame."

"Praise the Lord," shouted Reverend Petri.

"Make the blind see."

"Hail Jesus," added the Reverend. "Can you really do that?"

Petri looked around nervously.

"I only say this because we have to be careful, son. I do not claim to heal anyone. It is God who heals. And faith. If you believe..."

"I believe a demonstration is in order," said Devon as he started to enter the tent with Gordon right behind him. "Hey!" shouted Reverend Petri. "Wait. What are you doing?"

Devon and Gordon walked up to the first few rows where the crippled, the blind and the terminally ill sat, fanning themselves in the heat of the night. Devon nodded to Gordon, who pulled out his instrument just as Reverend Petri caught up with them.

"You just can't..."

Gordon strummed the strings on his instrument, filling the tent with a soothing spiritual melody that could lift the heart. Reverend Petri stared at Gordon.

"That's real nice, but I'm afraid I'm gonna have to ask you to leave," said the Reverend. "We don't carry insurance for this kind of..."

Gordon pointed the instrument at an older woman in a mobile bed, who was attached to a life support system. "No. Don't!" pleaded the Reverend.

Gordon strummed a beautiful chord that sent ripples through her body, lifting her off the bed on a wave of sound and then just as softly lowered her back down. Petri covered his eyes then looked to see what had happened.

The woman removed the IV tubes from her arms and got off her bed. She looked down at herself in wonder and then began to dance. She danced all around the front of the tent.

Reverend Petri stared at the woman and then looked over at Devon and Gordon, his mouth wide open. He closed his mouth and walked over to them. "Okay. Whatever the trick is, it worked. I've seen the masters, boy, but your friend is the best. Okay. Sixty-forty split on the collection."

Gordon was still watching the old woman dance when Devon joined him. "We're all set," said Devon. "This is the beginning of something great. I can feel it."

"There's just one problem," said Gordon.

"What?"

"I can't do it."

As Reverend Petri stepped up to the pulpit to get his congregation ready, Devon pulled Gordon aside. "Now what?" asked Devon.

"Why don't I just call the FBI and tell 'em to come get me?"

"Huh?"

"Whatta ya think? Suddenly this dude shows up in the South healing people with music. The Feds'll be here before you can say J. Edgar Hoover. I'm sorry Devon."

"You want to wimp out on me, fine. If you're too scared, teach me how to do it," said Devon.

"It's not me I'm worried about. It's this," said Gordon, holding up his instrument. "I can't let the wrong people get their hands on this."

"We got away before. Come on. Look at these people. They need you."

Gordon looked out at the tent and saw more and more people arriving in wheelchairs, on stretchers, some in portable beds.

"Whatta ya gonna do? Go back on the road with some heavy metal boneheads?"

"At least nobody shot at me," said Gordon. "Worst thing there was a few boos and hisses. I'm really a coward at heart, Devon."

"Keep telling yourself that, Gordon. Don't bull-shit me. I saw you stand up to those FBI guys. No, you're not a coward. But you are just like every other adult I've ever known. Just one big disappointment. All talk and no walk. When things get tough you're gone. Well if that's what I've gotta look forward to, then the hell with ya. You don't deserve that instrument."

Devon turned and started to walk away.

"Wait," said Gordon. Devon stopped and turned around. "This is it. The last time."

Devon smiled. Just then Janice, Huddleson and Sharon hurried over to Devon and Gordon.

"This is your cover?" asked Huddleson. "A travel-ing salvation show?"

"Don't you start," said Devon.

"This is my last gig," said Gordon.

"A little young for retirement, aren't ya?" said Sharon.

Gordon gave Sharon a big wet kiss. He then looked around at all the sick and bed-ridden people. "Guess we oughta get started." Gordon adjusted his instrument as a thought registered on his smiling face. He lowered his instrument.

"What are you doing?" asked Devon, concerned.

"I'm gonna try something different," said Gordon.

"Different? How different?"

"Human voices."

Devon looked confused.

"You may not know it, but the purest instrument for sound is the human voice," said Gordon. "It just needs to be opened and mixed in the perfect harmonic blend."

Gordon picked up his instrument. He looked around and then hit a chord. He nodded to Janice.

"Janice, start humming along with the music."

Janice opened her mouth and began singing along with the music. Only it wasn't your normal vocal singing. It was sound and vibration singing. Her mouth opened and beautiful sound emerged. As Gordon pointed to each person in his group, Huddleson, Sharon and Devon, they too began to sing. Gordon aimed his instrument at each one and plucked a string just as each person opened their mouths and voice. It seemed as if each voice was tuned to a different pitch and that each person had been turned into an accompanying instrument, a human instrument, each blending in a majestic choir. When they sang together they sounded like a chorus of angels. The light inside the tent began to get brighter as Gordon aimed at each person there. Reverend Petri stared in wonder until he saw the instrument aimed at him and he, too, opened his mouth in song...

CHAPTER TWENTY-FOUR

B_riggs and Powell were_ in their government sedan driving down the highway with the Colonel in his Humvee right behind them. Powell looked back at the Humvee. "He tapped all their phones?"

"It worked, didn't it," said Briggs.

"We picked up his friends just south of Charlotte and followed them out here, though God knows why."

"We've got him surrounded, and this time, there aren't any roof tops to jump over," said Powell, as the car passed the revival billboard.

"Isn't this where they found the bus?"

"Yes, sir," said Powell as he turned down the narrow road. In the distance they could see a light glowing.

"What's that?" asked Briggs.

Powell lowered his window and smiled. "Hear it?"

"That don't sound like our boy," said Briggs.

"But it's him," said Powell as he hit the gas.

The choir was singing and Gordon was leading them like a conductor. He then turned to the assembled multitude and waved the instrument at them.

"Open up," shouted Gordon. "Open your voices. You can do it! You can heal yourselves!"

The convoy arrived outside the tent which seemed to be aglow in a bright heavenly light. Briggs got out of the car and stared at the spray of brightness coming from beneath the tent where it barely touched the ground.

Inside, the singing rose to a thundering crescendo and then ended with a soaring hallelujah-like climax. Gordon lowered his instrument and smiled proudly. The tent was still glowing and the people were, too. A blind man stood up and walked around without his seeing-eye dog. "I can see. I can see."

A man in a wheelchair looked around nervously and then stood, unassisted. A young boy pulled a sling off of his arm. Reverend Petri approached Gordon, who handed the instrument to Devon. Devon looked at the instrument admiringly.

"You gotta teach me how to play this thing."

"Then they can shoot at you."

"Brother...ah I didn't get your name."

Just then the crowd moved apart as Briggs walked through holding a gun in his hand aimed directly at Gordon.

"Show's over, folks," said Briggs.

Gordon looked at Briggs and smiled. He then looked at Devon, who was still holding the instrument. Army troops surrounded the tent as the Colonel joined Briggs.

"Colonel Pemberton?" said Gordon.

"Hello, Gordon," replied the Colonel.

"He knows your name?" Devon said to Gordon. "How come he knows your name?"

"Your extraterrestrial, son, is a naughty boy," said the Colonel.

Devon looked at Gordon. "What's going on?"

"Shall I tell him, Gordon, or will you?"

"Tell me what?"

"Mr. Gordon is a very sick man."

Devon moved closer to Gordon. "What's he talking about?"

Gordon took his instrument back from Devon and the soldiers took aim.

"No!" shouted the Colonel. "Gordon, just put the weapon down. It's all over."

Devon looked at the instrument with a confused expression on his face. "What weapon?"

"It's government property," said Colonel Pemberton.

Devon looked at Gordon. "What's he saying?"

"Dr. Gordon is with us, Devon," said the Colonel. "Or at least he was."

"I don't understand," said Devon.

"Dr. Gordon is a physicist working for DARPA. Defense Advanced Research Projects Agency. It's under the Defense Department."

"What?"

"Dr. Gordon specializes in experimental weapons."

A pained look crossed Devon's face as he stared at Gordon, who shook his head.

"He discovered a way to tap into the power of sound," continued Pemberton. "He was developing a way to use this power in a new line of weaponry when he...well, went over the edge."

"Don't believe him, Devon," pleaded Gordon. "That's not what happened. I never went over any edge."

"You destroyed the laboratory," said Pemberton. "You stole government property. And you nearly killed a half-dozen people. Does that sound like normal behavior to you?"

"I also showed you how sound heals," said Gordon, "only nobody at the agency wanted to hear about that. NO! All you cared about was how well it could destroy. How well it could kill, and immobilize. To you it's just a cost-efficient, light-weight, low-power instrument of mass destruction."

"We'll get you help," said Colonel Pemberton.

Devon glared at Gordon with his mouth open. "You lied to me! You're not an alien?"

"I never really said I was," replied Gordon. "You gave me that tag. I just went along with it because, well, why not?"

"It's not uncommon, why you snapped," said Pemberton. "In fact, the same thing happened to the men who invented the first atom bomb. Caught in a moral dilemma, the mind shuts down, turns inward, and eventually you become a paranoid schizophrenic."

"Wait, you mean people aren't really chasing me and shooting at me?" said Gordon.

"Devon," urged Colonel Pemberton. "Why don't

you come over here? At this point, we still consider you a kidnap victim."

Devon turned toward Gordon. "So all this time, you were just using me."

"If you can't use your friends, who can you use?" quipped Gordon.

"Friends tell each other the truth," said Devon.

"Actually, I did," said Gordon.

"Oh yeah, when?"

"Devon, Dr. Gordon is mentally disturbed. Whatever he told you was probably some kind of delusional fantasy. But he also happens to be a genius. We thought we could control him. And we could—as long as he took his medication. Only he stopped. That's when the trouble started."

"He's lying, Devon," insisted Gordon. "I was never on any medication."

Devon looked torn. He didn't know who to believe anymore.

"You want to see the report? He had a psychotic break over how to use the sound force," said Colonel Pemberton.

"I'd call it more of a moral disagreement," said Gordon. "They want me to blow things up and I want to make things better. Creative differences."

"But you already blew up a couple of buildings when you stole our weapon," said Pemberton. "You see, Devon, even he doesn't know what he wants to do with his gift. He could turn on you any second."

Devon thought about what the Colonel was saying. "I know. I've seen it."

Gordon lowered his head, ashamed.

"The weapon," Pemberton ordered. "Now, please."

The FBI and Army personnel took positions around the tent, their weapons trained on Gordon.

"It's all over, Doctor," said Pemberton. "Just put down the weapon before someone gets hurt."

"Devon," said Gordon.

"What?"

"It's your call," said Gordon.

"My call? How is it my call?"

"Because I trust your instincts," said Gordon.

"You do?"

"You've been right so far."

"You must really be crazy," said Devon.

Gordon ran a finger along the neck of the instrument.

A thousand triggers cocked in one loud *click*.

"Just put it down," ordered Pemberton.

CHAPTER TWENTY-FIVE

With FBI agents and National Guard soldiers aiming at him, Gordon quickly let his finger slip over the strings while his other hand strummed a B-sharp that sent a shudder through the tent, causing poles to buckle and fold, and the huge canvas to collapse, causing panic and confusion.

Soldiers and agents stared at their useless weapons that had locked and refused to fire.

"Don't let him get away," shouted Briggs as he watched a figure trying to duck under the tent. He aimed his magnum and pulled the trigger but nothing happened. Like every other rifle and pistol in the vicinity, it had jammed from the instrument's metallic-sounding vibration.

Gordon was pushing Devon under the falling canvas until they were outside the fluttering tent. "Huddleson said he'd rented a red Toyota. It's gotta be around here somewhere," said Devon.

"You go on," said Gordon.

"It's not me they're after," said Devon.

"Good point," said Gordon as a shot rang out. Gordon's eyes widened as he looked down and saw a red hole appear in his side.

"How?" But that was all Gordon was able to spit

out when he fell to the ground.

"You've been shot!" shouted Devon.

"I did it," called a soldier. "Colonel, it worked. I hit him."

Colonel Pemberton walked up to the soldier and took a weapon from him that was made of solid wood. "Good man."

Briggs ran to Pemberton to see how the Colonel was able to accomplish what the FBI had not. The Colonel was holding the weapon proudly.

"No sense in developing a weapon if you can't create a counter weapon to fight it," said the Colonel. "We're the Army, Special Agent Briggs, ready for any contingency."

Devon looked over at Pemberton and bent down to help Gordon stand up. "Come on Gordon, we can still get out of here."

Huddleson joined them and put another arm under Gordon's other side. "Let me help," said Huddleson.

"Go get your car," pleaded Devon. "I've got him."

Huddleson ran into the sea of vehicles as Devon half-carried and half-pulled Gordon into the stampeding crowd of revivalists. It wasn't long before a Toyota Highlander pulled up with Huddleson behind the wheel. Sharon was in the passenger seat and Janice in the rear.

"Open the back," Devon said tersely. Janice lowered her seat and Huddleson pulled a latch that opened the rear door of the SUV. Devon pushed and Janice pulled Gordon, still clutching the instrument, into the vehicle as Huddleson gave it some gas and maneuvered through the crowd.

Briggs followed the Colonel into the crowd. The Colonel had locked and loaded the wooden rifle. Briggs put his weapon away as it had been rendered basically useless. It was then he saw the blood on the ground. "There. They went that way."

"He's hit bad," said the Colonel. "He won't get very far."

Devon had Gordon lying on the folded-down back seat of the Highlander. Janice stared at Gordon's wound and made a face. "That doesn't look too good," she said.

Gordon was about to pass out when Devon slapped his face, bringing him back to consciousness.

"Hey," said Gordon. "You hit me."

"You can't pass out," said Devon. "You have to tell me what to do."

"It's not that easy."

"Just tell me what to do," begged Devon.

"Don't let him die," pleaded Sharon from the passenger seat.

Gordon shifted a little and winced in pain. "Man. I've never been shot before. This really hurts."

"Will you shut up and tell me what to do?"

Janice looked out the window and saw that helicopters were following the car overhead. She then looked behind them and saw a convoy of troops giving chase in trucks, government sedans and police cars.

Devon picked up the instrument and studied its features. It looked like a fancy electric guitar with extra bells and whistles. There were knobs and dials, and levers. Devon shook his head.

"If you're not gonna tell me, I'll just have to try it for myself," said Devon.

"How do propose to do that?" asked Gordon.

"I can play the guitar, a little. Isn't that what this is? Just a fancy guitar?"

Devon strummed a sour note and pain shot through Gordon's body.

"Agggghhhh!" screamed Gordon.

Huddleson looked back and exchanged a worried glance with Devon.

"Sorry," said Devon.

"Do you know any chords?" asked Gordon, still wincing.

"A few," said Devon.

"A-major?"

"I think so," said Devon as he placed his fingers on the strings over the frets and strummed with his other hand.

"That's it," said Gordon. "Do it again."

Devon strums the chord again.

"Now give me a full G."

Devon shifted his fingers and strummed another chord.

"Oooo, yeah. D-7."

Devon strummed that that one.

"Oh yeah. Okay, now repeat that progression. A-major, G, D-7. Just keep repeating it."

Devon ran through the chords again and again and before long he realized that he was playing an old rock classic, "That'll be the Day."

"Play it, Dev, baby. Play it," smiled Gordon.

With each strum, the wound on Gordon's side began to heal a little more until it had completely vanished. Devon stopped strumming and Gordon looked at him. "Don't stop."

Devon continued to play and Gordon sat up and began swaying. Sharon climbed over the seat and crawled to him and began hugging him as Gordon and Devon continued singing, "...*that'll be the day*..."

Devon smiled at Janice, who took his head in her hands and kissed him on the mouth.

"Yeah, Devon," shouted Gordon.

Suddenly a helicopter swooped down in front of the SUV and Huddleson hit the brakes.

"Stop the vehicle," ordered an amplified, stern male voice from inside the chopper.

"We're all gonna die!' shouted Janice as the Highlander skidded toward the side of the road.

Gordon stopped hugging Sharon and took the instrument away from Devon.

"Wanta see what this baby was really made for?" asked Gordon.

Devon smiled.

Gordon rolled down the window and aimed the neck of the instrument outside.

The pilot looked down and saw the neck of the instrument sticking out the back window.

"What the hell is that?" asked the pilot.

His passenger, the Colonel, looked down wide-eyed. "I guess his wound wasn't that bad. You better back away, quickly."

Gordon strummed a sour note that jolted the car and rippled through the air at the chopper, just missing it as it banked away.

The ripple created a wall of air that the following cars smashed into. The lead car plunged into the invisible shield, crumbling up as if by magic.

Another helicopter, unaware of the invisible wall, slammed into it, but didn't crash. Instead, the chopper plunged into the air which was no longer hard but a soft fluffy mass that caused the chopper to slowly drop out of the sky on a pillow of air.

Colonel Pemberton looked at the other chopper. His helicopter landed as soldiers and policemen ran up against the invisible wall as it slowly disappeared.

"Come on. Go after them!" shouted the Colonel. But when the Humvees and armored vehicles started to follow the SUV the road in front of them rose up with a ripping sound as pavement was pulled from gravel and ground until it buckled in a mangled mound of blacktop.

The Colonel threw down his hat as Briggs approached him.

"Well played, Colonel," snickered Briggs. "Ready for any contingency, heh?"

"It would have been a great weapon," sighed the Colonel.

✦

T*he Toyota Highlander* continued to speed down the highway leaving the Army and FBI far behind. Devon looked back until he was sure they were no longer being followed. Only then, he felt himself relax and let out a deep breath. He looked back to see Gordon in Sharon's caring arms snuggling against her chest, his eyes closed and a smile on his mouth. As the SUV continued on down the road, Devon thought about everything he had learned.

Gordon was as human as he was. But he had been so certain that what he had been communicating with was of another world. He felt like the world's biggest fool. How was ever going to face the kids back at school, or his parents? As he wrestled within his different outcomes, he began to drift off, exhausted from the events of the last few hours.

W*hen Devon opened his* eyes, day had turned into night and the Highlander was stopped along the side of the road in the middle of nowhere. Cornfields stretched in every direction on both sides of the two-lane highway. The night sky was filled with stars. The others were outside sitting on a bank when Devon climbed out of the car and joined them.

"Where are we?" asked Devon. "Why did we stop?"

Gordon stood up smiling and approached Devon.

"This is where I say goodbye," said Gordon.

"You want to get out here? Why?"

"It's a perfect pick-up spot," said Gordon. "It's time to go home, Devon."

"So we'll take you there," said Devon.

"Oh, Devon," said Gordon, shaking his head. "Ya know, this is why I never made any friends. Good-byes are sons of bitches."

"So don't say goodbye. Whatever it is, we'll deal with it. You need a good lawyer, that's all."

"If only that were true," said Gordon. "I have to go. Gotta file a report. I'm gonna catch hell as it is for getting involved."

"My Dad knows some really good attorneys. We can get you help."

"You're a good boy, Devon."

Gordon put out his hand to shake but Devon just stared at it.

"No. This isn't right," insisted Devon.

"I'll try to keep in touch. Besides, I gotta feeling they're gonna send me back here someday to tie up loose ends. Goodbye, Devon. Thanks for every-thing."

Gordon put his hand on Devon's shoulder and then pulled him to his chest and gave him a big hug. Gordon pulled away and wiped a tear from his eye as he started to walk off into the night.

"Wait. Who are 'they'? Where are you going?"

Devon started to walk after him when the night sky lit up in a brilliant pattern of light and sound. It looked like the aurora borealis of the Northern Lights. Devon and the others looked up and through some low hanging clouds appeared the bottom of some kind of airship. Most of it was concealed in cloud-cover. A bright cone of light beamed down from an opening and Gordon stepped into the light. He turned around and looked at Gordon and waved once. Suddenly the light disappeared, leaving the cornfield in darkness. Devon ran to where Gordon was standing but no one was there. Then Devon looked down at the ground and lying there among the tall grass was the instrument. Devon stared at it wide-eyed as Janice, Huddleson and Sharon joined him.

They all looked skyward together as the cloud began to move across the night sky until it vanished over the horizon.

Janice was the first to speak. "Wait," she said. "You mean he really is an alien?"

A cool breeze swooped in from the east bending the tall cornstalks and one by one, Devon, Janice, Huddleson and Sharon fell to the ground, unconscious.

The sun was rising just as Devon opened his eyes. He looked down and saw that his left hand was holding the neck of Gordon's instrument. As he rose up slowly, the others, too, began to regain consciousness.

Janice rubbed her eyes. "Wow, did I have the most amazing dream."

Professor Huddleson looked around at the cornfield and then at Devon and Janice. "What am I doing here?" He studied Devon curiously. "Wait. I know you from somewhere." He then noticed

Sharon, who had a confused expression on her face as well. "Who are you?" asked Huddleson.

Devon shook his head and gazed at the guitar-like instrument. He then looked up at the sky and slowly began to smile.

CHAPTER TWENTY-SIX

Two months later, back at the Alpine, New Jersey schoolyard where classes had just ended for the day, Devon was walking to his bike when a government sedan pulled up. The rear door opened and Colonel Pemberton climbed out. Devon started to unlock his bike as the Colonel approached him.

"Devon, how are you doing today?" asked Pemberton.

"No different than yesterday, or the day before that," replied Devon. "I still don't know why you keep coming by. I've told you a million times, I don't know what you're talking about."

"No word from our friend, I take it?"

"Nope. Not that I even know who it is you're referring to."

"This amnesia game is getting a little tired, don't you think?" said Pemberton.

"Then stop bothering me," said Devon.

"It's a shame, isn't it?"

"What is?"

"That a man with his talent has to live his life on the run," said the Colonel.

"If you say so," said Devon, climbing onto his bike.

"We'll catch him, you know," said the Colonel with certainty, "as soon as he starts playing with that toy of his. So, you take care now, son."

"Right." Devon gave the Colonel a salute and began to pedal away, leaving the Colonel leaning against his black sedan.

Devon turned a corner and when he felt safe enough, he pulled his bike over and leaned it against a well-trimmed bush. He then reached into his backpack and pulled out a magazine. It was the latest issue of the *New England Journal of Medicine*.

He opened it to a page marked with a yellow post-it note. The title of the article read: "Physicist discovers how to manipulate the weather" and under the article headline in hand-written scrawl was a note.

"*Dear Devon. Thought you'd get a kick out of this. I've been reassigned to a liberal arts college in Maine, where I've been working with the physics department. It's a lot better than that think-tank gig. By the time you read this, however, I'll be gone, since I'm told the FBI and the Army intelligence also knows how to read.*

"*Sorry about that memory swipe with your friends but I have to maintain a low profile. As for the cloud cover, I used to work on stealth applications of meteorological phenomenon. I kind of overstepped the boundaries by connecting with you but that concert was just too hard to resist. Hey I'm only human, (well, sort of). You have the tool now so put it to good use.*

"*I've reprogrammed the frequencies slightly in*

case Colonel Pemberton thinks he'll be able to lock on to it if you start playing it. It should be safe for awhile, anyway. Meanwhile, keep up your music lessons. Be good, my friend, and keep your eyes on the sky. You never know when I'll be in the neighborhood and want to jam. Hasta lavista, baby. —Gordon."

It *was nearing sundown* as Devon entered his house and found his parents arguing.

"It's over, Anita," said Arnold. "Just sign the papers."

"Fine," she replied bitterly. "The sooner the better."

"Hi, Mom. Dad."

They both turned toward Devon with expressions of shame on their faces.

"Devon," said Anita. "I'm sorry you had to hear this."

"He's heard it all before," said Arnold.

"Damn you," she yelled. "Get out of this house."

"Don't worry," said Arnold. "I'm gone."

Arnold was heading for the door when a realization crossed Devon's face. He looked at his father. "Dad," said Devon. "Could you just hold on a second?"

"What now?"

"Just wait there. I'll be right back."

Devon ran up the stairs as Arnold glared at his wife.

Devon entered his bedroom and went to his

closet.

Arnold and Anita had resumed fighting when Devon returned.

"My fault?" shouted Arnold. "It's always my fault. The hell with this. Devon! I'm sorry, son, but I can't stay here any longer. I'm leaving. Goodbye."

Arnold picked up his suitcase and reached for the door when Devon adjusted the instrument he was carrying down the stairs.

"Dad, wait," said Devon, as he began to strum the instrument. "There's something I'd like you to hear."

"I'm sorry Devon; I don't have time to..."

Arnold turned to open the front door when Devon strummed the instrument again and this time the "music" lit up the room. Arnold stopped and turned. The scowl on Arnold's face was replaced by a warm smile as he put down his suitcase. He turned to his wife as she came into his arms and they looked at each in a way they hadn't in a long time. They were glowing.

Devon strummed the instrument, creating a loving melody. As he strummed he happened to glance down at a newspaper sitting on a table.

The headline read: "Funds Needed to Expand Children's Cancer Hospital."

Arnold and Anita were about to kiss when the slamming of a screen door interrupted their reverie. They turned toward the door.

"Devon?" said Arnold.

"Shhhh," said Anita as she stood on her toes and put her lips on her husband's.

✦

T*he entrance to the* ward for children being treated for cancer swung open as someone entered wearing a hospital orderly uniform. Visiting hours had ended and the ward was starting to wind down. Every bed was filled with bald children watching television sets mounted over their beds.

The orderly pushed a food cart down the middle of the ward until he came to Billy's bed. Billy was the boy Devon had seen during his first visit to this ward. Tonight Billy was looking particularly sad and drawn. He glanced up at the person in the orderly uniform.

It was Devon. He placed a food tray next to the Billy's bed and then sat down beside him.

"How are you feeling today?"

"Not so good," said Billy. "You know, I already ate."

"That's okay," said Devon. "I'm not really here for the food."

"You're not gonna throw up again, are ya?"

"I hope not," said Devon, who then reached under the food cart and pulled out the instrument. Billy gave him a perplexed look.

"What's that?" asked Billy.

"How'd you like to hear a little music?" asked Devon.

"Music?"

"Unfortunately, I only know a couple of tunes," said Devon. "Ever heard of Buddy Holly?"

"Buddy who?"

"He was before my time, too. It doesn't matter," said Devon, as he began to strum the chords of "That'll be the Day." The whole ward lit up in a heavenly glow.

ABOUT THE AUTHOR

FRED YAGER is the author of the technothrillers *Rex* and *Cybersona* and the co-author, with Jan Yager, of the suspense novels *Untimely Death* and *Just Your Everyday People*. He was a reporter for the Associated Press for 13 years covering everything from politics and entertainment to general news and crime. He also worked at CBS News and Fox Television. A member of the Writers Guild of America, several of his screenplays have been optioned. Fred is also co-author of two reference books: *Career Opportunities in the Publishing Industry* and *Career Opportunities in the Film Industry*.

The author grew up in a small town in upstate New York, and, after serving in the U.S. Navy, moved to Manhattan. He and his wife Jan relocated to Fairfield County, Connecticut to raise their family; they have resided there for the last two decades.